Son

JULIA HAMILTON

A novel of Edward IV

SPHERE BOOKS LIMITED
30/32 Gray's Inn Road, London WC1X 8JL

First published in Great Britain in 1973
by Sphere Books Ltd

ACKNOWLEDGEMENTS

My thanks to the London Library and to the Head Librarian of Bangor Public Library, Mr. W. J. Jones, for generous assistance given in the discovery of research books necessary for the writing of this biographical novel.

Set in Baskerville Intertype

Printed in Great Britain by
Hazell Watson & Viney Ltd
Aylesbury, Bucks

ISBN 0 7221 4286 2

The wolf breaks and tugs at the Crown
With fang and claw;
The lion, full of wrath,
Smites him with his paw.

John Petit

Boast not, my lords, your gorgeous rings,
Fine horses, clothes and such like things.
Your retinue no profit brings
If prudence from its actions wings
        A speedy flight;
And boldness in an evil plight
        Is more than might.

Ramon Lull

The Rose won the victory, the field and also the chase;
Now may the husband in the South dwell in his own place;
His wife and eke his fair daughter, and all the good he has;
Such means hath the Rose made, by virtue and by grace.
Blessed be the time, that ever God sprad that flower!

The Rose come to London, full royally riding,
Two archbishops of England they crowned the Rose King;
Almighty Jesu, save the Rose, and give him His blessing,
And all the realm of England joy of his crowning.

Written at the time of the coronation
of Edward IV, the 'Rose of Rouen'

Also in this series and available in Sphere Books

VICTORIA by Evelyn Anthony
AN UNKNOWN WELSHMAN by Jean Stubbs
THE SPANISH TUDOR by Freda M. Long

Editorial adviser Julia Watson

CONTENTS

THE ANCESTRY OF EDWARD IV

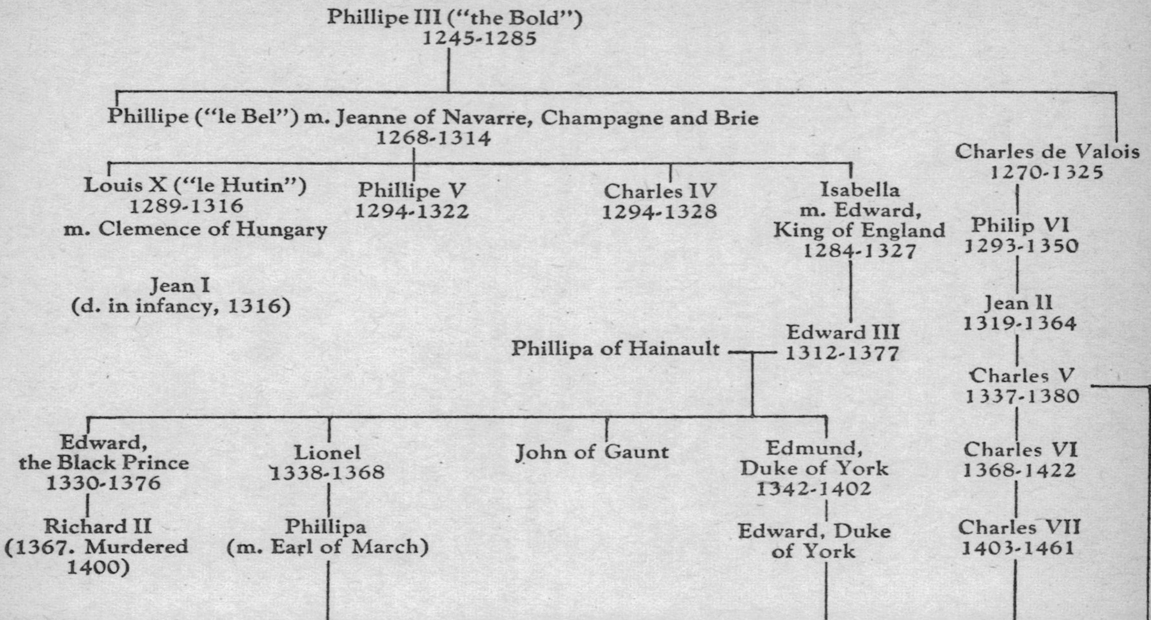

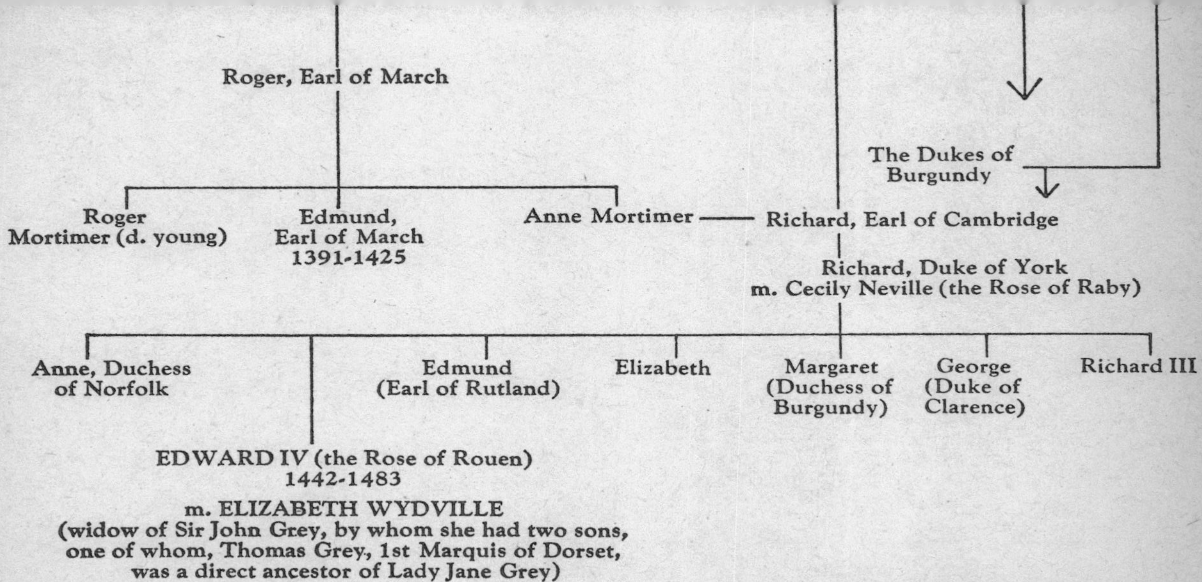
Roger, Earl of March
The Dukes of Burgundy
Roger Mortimer (d. young)
Edmund, Earl of March 1391-1425
Anne Mortimer
Richard, Earl of Cambridge
Richard, Duke of York m. Cecily Neville (the Rose of Raby)
Anne, Duchess of Norfolk
Edmund (Earl of Rutland)
Elizabeth
Margaret (Duchess of Burgundy)
George (Duke of Clarence)
Richard III
EDWARD IV (the Rose of Rouen) 1442-1483
m. ELIZABETH WYDVILLE
(widow of Sir John Grey, by whom she had two sons, one of whom, Thomas Grey, 1st Marquis of Dorset, was a direct ancestor of Lady Jane Grey)

ROYAL SUN UPON THE HORIZON, 1442–1447

I was born the third of a family of twelve, my father Richard Duke of York, my mother Cecily Neville, called the White Rose of Raby for her great beauty. My sister Anne was born three years before me, at Fotheringay in 1439, and Henry, too, but he died in infancy; then after me came the vivid brood, Edmund, born in 1443, Elizabeth, born in 1444, Margaret born in 1446, William (who died when a babe, as did John), George, born in 1449, Thomas, born in 1450, Richard, who arrived on October 2, 1452, and Ursula, the last, birthed in 1455, and so soon to die. Some were born at Rouen, as was I, others at Fotheringay, while Henry was born at Hatfield, John at Neath, and George in Dublin. These if naught else revealing our parents' proclivities for travel.

But Fotheringay was our home, the grey stone castle in Northamptonshire standing sturdy and solid beside the River Nen, raised upon a small mound in Norman style and with a high keep. Here our parents held lavish and merry court, as they so loved to do, and here came the jesters, the jugglers, the wrestlers, the play-actors, the minstrels, the troubadours and the dancers to exhibit their talents, entertain the second most important man in England next the King, and receive largesse for their pains. Wherever we went, my family and I, there was colour and action, excitement and adventure, whether we were resident at Fotheringay, Rouen or later at Dublin when my father was made Lieutenant-General of Ireland. (He had been Governor of Normandy until King Henry's marriage, but now was expected to cosset a lesser post without grumble, though he knew he had received it because of the Vixen-Queen's jealousy and her intimacy with Suffolk, his enemy.) Yet so superior a man was my father that he became greatly admired in Ireland, it being said that no Englishman had ever been so loved by the Irish; and later, when he needed assistance to assert his position in England against the Vixen-Queen, Margaret of Anjou, it was the eager Irish who scurried forward to back him.

The Vixen-Queen, daughter of René of Anjou, the artist-

King, and of Isabelle of Lorraine, who brought René the Duchy of Lorraine, had begun her reign in England as a radiant and charming sixteen-year-old, after becoming wife to the monkish Henry VI (he who was descended from Edward III as was my father, his line from John of Gaunt and ours from Edmund, Duke of York, and Lionel, Duke of Clarence.) Margaret, whose father had selected 'humble et loiall' for his adored daughter's motto, had pleased all England at first, impressing all with her talents (she spoke Spanish and Italian, read Greek, displayed a ready wit and danced like a nymph.) Had any man experienced a twinge of doubt concerning Margaret's suitability for the Monk-King Henry, he had but to consider Margaret's two grandmothers, Yolande of Aragon and Marguerite of Bavaria, both renowned for their piety. My mother often spoke to me of the Queen's early years in England, of how news of her beauty and wit surged through the land like wildfire, bringing gladness to all men's hearts. But all too soon the gladness was to be quenched, the great ruby which had been Margaret's marriage ring being the harbinger of the blood which later was to be shed because of her. For almost before she was crowned came scandal and witchery: Duke Humphrey,* my father's great friend, was robbed of his Protectorate and banished from the Privy Council, his wife, Eleanor Cobham being accused of sorcery and exiled to the Isle of Man. And then it was my father was recalled from France and despatched to Ireland.

In June, 1441, my father had taken ship for Normandy, accompanied by a great bevy of soldiers, later my mother Cecily following him laden with chests and carved furniture, tapestries and goblets to outfit the governor's mansion in Rouen. Great days those, burdened with promise and joy, and I daresay my mother soon relinquished her grief at the loss of the baby boy during the previous February. She was always one for new ventures and new delights, and never once did I hear her grumble at being swamped by chests and packages and harassed by children wherever we journeyed. But I was not yet born when she and my father arrived in Rouen, bursting with enthusiasm, strewing their apartments at Bouvreuil Castle with all the appendages of

* Humphrey, Duke of Gloucester, brother of Henry V.

court life, grasping the reins of rule tightly into their young and capable hands. Were it not for my father Normandy might have collapsed into French hands! Only a short time before, Jeanne d'Arc had been marching with her devoted French soldiers to thrust we English from Normandy, repeating her 'direct message from Heaven' that the English should and would be driven from French soil, her vacillating French King, Charles de Valois, malleable as an eel in her arms. In 1431, in Spring, she had been bound to a stake and put to the flames, and Charles had collapsed like a scarecrow from which ravening birds have plucked all the stuffing. From that day, the English had risen as if multiplied and strengthened by God's beneficence, being determined to cling on to those parts of France which they cherished, looking upon them as the farthest frontiers of England.

But it had not been easy. The siege, when Charles de Valois' army had attempted to take Pontoise for the French, had been only one problem to face; Guienne had been another, with the entire French army battling to commandeer the province. And desperate need for money had plagued my father all the while, for it seemed as if some gremlin in London would deny him both payment and recognition of his deeds, while John Beaufort was created King's Lieutenant and Captain-General of Guienne and given a handsome sum of £25,000 to bolster his task. My father at last was told to 'take patience and forbear for a while if wages in Rouen fall into arrear'. Even then, the King depended upon the popularity of the Duke of York to recompense his soldiers for going unpaid! But of course the King expected my father to finance the entirety of Normandy with Yorkist wealth and, knowing my father's straight and generous nature he had no doubt this would be done. God alone knew what state England was being driven into at that time by the arrogant Beauforts who manipulated young King Henry as though he were a moppet. The Beauforts, descended from Edward III through John of Gaunt by his union with Katherine Swynford,* had ever been lofty and avaricious, and now Cardinal Beaufort was lording it in

* His mistress while he was married to the Duchess Blanche and then to Constanza of Castile. Katherine Swynford married him towards the end of his life, and their children were made legitimate.

England energetically aided and abetted by the rest of his family. But the King was as yet unwed, and a bride must be found for him. Firstly, the Cardinal considered a bride from the Valois blood, then the daughter of the Count of Armagnac (which threw Normandy into a fury for they had been bravely fighting at their own expense against Valois, Armagnac and Burgundian). Meanwhile, John Beaufort, recently elevated to the Dukedom of Somerset, was allowing Normandy slowly to slide into French hands by dint of his misjudgement and total inability to command wisely. My father, who must take orders from him, could do naught but grieve in silence.

Then at last the bride was selected, she being Margaret, daughter of the King of Anjou, and the three who had selected her—thereby cursing England—were Cardinal Beaufort, his brother Edmund, and William de la Pole, whose wife was the Cardinal's niece. However, after Somerset's blunderings and botchings in Normandy, they could not risk another Beaufort disaster, and de la Pole was left to carry out the marriage negotiations alone.

I was two years old when Somerset crawled back to London leaving a rent and bruised Normandy behind him, to discover his King would not acknowledge him at court, and his wife would have none of him, she openly naming him fool and dolt. Their daughter Margaret was three years old at that time, no doubt the knowledge that her father was a witless creature ensuring she would strive for wisdom far in excess of her years. When Somerset, Duke of Misrule, died soon after, he was not mourned. Greedily, his equally inept brother, Edmund, took the title.

Then came Easter, 1445, and with it the new bride chosen for young King Henry, and Rouen was brash with colour and tapestry to welcome the beautiful Princess who would prove to be a monstrous Circe, Goddess-Witch. My parents entertained her royally, and I have never discovered what took place between them (other than kindly formalities) which made Margaret of Anjou so hate and detest them ever after. Yet she was ever given to sudden, swift and unreasoning prejudices was the Circe-Queen, born under the sign of Mars, Bringer of War and Chaos, this wild impulsive need for hating engendering her downfall, and that of her husband and her son. (Had it not been for my father, England's downfall too.) Margaret, with her dense witch-black hair and glittering eyes and that powerful strength of spirit which was entirely too much for one person to contain and she a woman at that, was later found to have been accepted for her beauty alone, for she came to Henry *dowerless*. Her father, it appeared, had burnt out his wealth in wars and shows of extravagance and high pomp. We English, desperately desirous of money, felt wickedly cheated, and the Beauforts were loved even less when it became common knowledge Margaret of Anjou brought no gold with her. From the first, though so young, there were those who declared her too haughty for English tastes, yet others were eager to praise the beauty who was now become Queen. Suffolk, for one, who was the King's proxy for the marriage service, openly adored her, and she lavished excessive favour upon him. How innocent her emblem must have seemed, the dainty white frilled daisy, demure and sweet! Only later was it remembered how the daisy grew and how speedily it throttled England's healthy greenery! A pretty weed which proliferates and suffocates where it grows unhindered.

Had young Henry been stronger and more of a man, she would have been kept in check, but he was a muddle-headed monk, suffering from the purulent heritage of his French grandfather, Charles VI, and that purulence was insanity, a strange, milked version which had sprung up slowly in Henry V's son. When he was small it was nothing more than a mildness where other boys flung themselves about and were eager to practise at the butts, but as he grew it became a vacuousness which altogether was untenable in a King who must be his country's strength. And now at twenty-four he was milder than any monk and more vacuous than any fool, and there were other tales to add to the unpleasantness: a Kentish yeoman was arrested for loudly declaring that "the King is a lunatic as his grandsire was" and Henry, stupidly, had bestowed the Stewardship of Cornwall upon two men simultaneously! Then there were the other rumours: those which said the King was impotent, could never sire an heir however much he should desire to, and that he had no lust for his lovely young bride but preferred spying upon his courtiers in their more intimate moments to throwing himself into the disordered and lusty entanglements of the marriage bed.

There is a sentence from the Bible which says, 'Woe to thee O Land, when thy King is a child!' and, even at twenty-four, there was no sign Henry had reached mental maturity.

So the Vixen-Queen was despatched to London, where she remained as virgin as she had been in Rouen, and my father's term of Governorship ended. By this time Henry, child or no child, owed my father £38,000 and, after returning to England, he had no recourse but to forget twelve thousand of that, and accept tallies for the remaining £26,000, tallies which he believed would be exchangeable for coin one day in the near future. But, goodly-natured and trusting as he ever was, my father was shortly to realise many unpleasantries, the main being that his advice was unwelcome in the King's Council despite his importance, and that there was some secret collusion from which he was totally excluded. At last it came out: the horror which was part and parcel of the marriage treaty between Margaret of Anjou's father and the King of England. Not only had the Vixen-Queen come dowerless to London, but her impoverished father—as part of his agreement to part with her—had been promised England's beloved possessions in France: Anjou and Maine, which lands had been dearly purchased with the blood of many and good Englishmen!

Small wonder Margaret of Anjou was looked upon in harsh new light for, with all her beauty, wit and elegance, she was not the equivalent in English eyes of beloved Anjou and Maine, hewed from French hands by Henry V of Agincourt, our Hero-King. Treasured lands, and she but a fragile form of flesh and bones, a young girl with fortune to own a beauteous face! Yet by this juncture, addle-craniumed Henry VI was so enamoured of his *belle* bride that she could not say or do an ill thing in his eyes (though for all its depth, his worship was fleshless and chaste as a prior's). Then indeed she seemed to have little wrong with her; she was lovely and she was obedient: only the acute prejudices so inexplicably roused heralded the woman to come. It was not until she whelped, bringing forth Edward called Prince of Wales that the true Vixen stepped forward from the folds of silk and gauze, forsaking the feminine smiles and charming allure of the young bride. Then were men eager to recall she was born under the sign of Mars, Bringer of War and Discord, and oftentimes lust. And when we heard of Henry's bewilderment on viewing his son, and his remark that the child was seeded by the Holy Ghost but surely not by him? that we realised the long-barren Queen had sought elsewhere for her child's father. The 'Prince' revealed no sign of the purulent French inheritance nor of King Henry's weakly frame, but was a dark-haired, comely lad—and gifted too—with a fair quantity of intelligence. He did not in any manner resemble his hero-grandsire, Henry V, nor did the King acknowledge him. But that is further on in the story, and shall be related later.

Stupefied with the knowledge that their King's French wife had been bought with their French lands, further scandals broke in upon our ears. Gloucester, whom Margaret had ever hated for he had opposed her marriage and detested her homeland, had been discovered plotting to kill the King and snatch the Throne. To memory of his wife's recent banishment for witchcraft and the burning of her two accomplices, Margery Jourdaine and Roger Bolingbroke, was added news of Gloucester's perfidy, brought to the King and Queen by Cardinal Beaufort. The result of this was the Duke's arrest and his disappearance from the colour and turmoil of the city. Following this act, there were plans for a trial but soon came the announcement that the prisoner had died from a stroke, his corpse being exhibited to public view where no mark showed upon him. It had not been difficult to gather men eager to vote against the Duke, Owen Tudor, widower of Catherine de Valois, being one, and the Cliffords and the Percys, but the Duke's popularity with the Londoners had made it necessary to have him tried without the city, and for this Bury was chosen. When the Duke's death reached London ears, who could fail to suspect murder? Yet what method had been used? No one could say, for the King's uncle and late Protector of the Realm lay as one who had died peacefully in his bed. His bier was in Parliament's great hall where scores came to gaze upon him, and the talk was of poison, of strangling and suffocation by night, and of Edward II's obscene death.* The voices which recalled the Duke's previous attacks of sickness, and the likelihood of his having died from a cracked heart were barely heeded.

Then shortly after, the ancient Cardinal Beaufort, who had been a second father to the Vixen-Queen, snatched his burial shrouds in his gnarled hands and made for Purgatory. We heard he had stumbled about his Palace muttering, "Why should I die, having so much riches: if the whole realm would save my life, I am either by policy to get it or by riches buy it. Fie, will not death be hired, nor will money do nothing?" Now upon the scene there remained but two enemies for the Queen's favourite, Suffolk, to fight: Somerset, vain and foolish, impetuous and devoid of strategy, and my own father, Richard of York, married to Cecily, of the powerful Neville brood, its chief member the Earl of Salisbury who was planning to marry his son to the daughter of the Earl of Warwick.

Suffolk believed he dealt ably with them, for Edmund, the new Duke of Somerset, was made Regent of France (where he lost us our lands and wrought havoc) and my father was made Governor of Ireland at thirty-six—which post he was to fill for a decade. Their departure made William de la Pole, Earl of Suffolk, the mightiest man in England. The year was 1447.

* Edward II was murdered most horribly at Pontefract Castle, by order of his wife, Isabella de Valois, and her lover, Roger Mortimer.

MARS IN THE ASCENDANT, Spring, 1447–1450

Spring 1447 saw Margaret of Anjou coming fully into power. Her remarkable energy which many said was Devil-bred caused her to interfere with every item of England, both minute and enormous, with its governing and its policy and, each time her husband wrote to the French King, she too would write a letter to accompany his; whilst, lording it over the Queen, was Suffolk the soldier-adviser, and her two new Premiers: Lord Say, Suffolk's confidant, and the Bishop of Chichester, Cardinal Kemp.

There was no Salic Law in England to hinder this ambitious Queen, she being only one of many Queens who came from France to find their destiny beside an English King. From William the Conqueror to Henry VI, only two English heirs-Royal had married English wives: Edward the Black Prince and Henry IV. Others had gathered wives from Hainault and Bohemia, from Anjou and from Louvaine, from Aquitaine and Scotland. Here in England, unhampered and adulated as the Vixen-Queen was, her weed-roots were allowed to spring and creep and throttle her husband's Kingdom, whilst my father and his followers were expected to stand by with fatuous smiles upon their faces.

Now, added to the insult of the Vixen's marriage treaty, and her lewd favouring of Suffolk was the horror of Gloucester's sudden and mysterious death. Those who had once praised her very name now spoke of her with loathing and contempt. Yet more was to come. The King of France was the Vixen's uncle, and would not let her forget it. Instead of rebuffing his efforts to entangle her and thereby entangle England, she plunged into contact with him. Charles de Valoi's army had recently tasted victory in Switzerland and was now heading for Le Mans, which place the soldiers snatched successfully in 1448. Further fury assailed England, the Vixen hastily arranging for those who owned land in Maine to be indemnified by her husband—this proving a chill and worthless arrangement, for the treasury was naked of coin, and Parliament rebelled when ordered to vote taxes.

Suffolk had no recourse but to barter bishoprics, thereby gaining yet more dislike from the people, and thoroughly alienating the long-suffering clergy who saw their careers in great danger if religious titles could be bought by those whose only vocation was greed accompanied by sufficient gold.

And while England was misruled and led astray, Charles of France—imbecile that he was—saw his own coffers filling and his Kingdom flourishing. He was inept and ignorant, but his ministers, Jacques Coeur, Dunois, Richemont, Brézé, and Tancarville were rapidly giving him the name 'Charles the Well-Served', their country becoming richer and stronger than England whilst our Treaty with France was reaching its finale. Charles, with his optimistic army, could foresee his enemies defeated and brought low, for there was only Normandy and its paucity of soldiers to defend England's property in France. Suffolk, hated and abhorred, believed he could beg for help from Parliament but it was he whom they wished to conquer, and his attempt was futile. Shortly, after skirmishes and tangled fruitless arguments, the French snatched Verneuil, Valogne, Pont de l'Arche, and Upper and Lower Normandy, and had designs to claim more, even the Duke of Burgundy being eager to appropriate his share of the spoils. When we heard that more land was taken, Lisieux, Louviers, Gournay, Evreux, and Mantes, we wept and I, eight years old, heard that my birthplace Rouen, was under violent siege.

Somerset's blundering and now Suffolk's unpopularity had done their work well : the country which my father had strengthened and held for the English Crown with courage and pride was now embraced by the French *mêlée*. I recall my nurse Anne de Caux and I hearing that Rouen was besieged, and how we had stared white-cheeked at one another.

"They shall not stop at Rouen," Anne said, struggling to retain her tears.

"Where, then?" I asked.

"They shall fight through France and across the Channel and besiege us in England. Every castle, every city will be under siege. I know it!" Her voice seemed to crackle as though fingers gripped her throat.

Although I in the manly superiority of my eight years

knew her talk to be a woman's wild exaggeration, a stab of fear struck through my mind. I saw as if they really loomed before me the banners and emblems of the French, their soldiers marching beneath them, triumphant, London possessed by Valois, Burgundian, Armagnac, each party backing at our sweet city, burning and plundering, destroying and pillaging. The shudder which assailed me was almost too violent for me to hide from my nurse, yet whatever I did I must not put more fear in her for I was her charge and companion and she and I were alone at Ludlow, my parents being in Ireland and our sisters and brothers either with them or being educated in other households as was the custom. Anne, two years my senior, was to become betrothed to Exeter's heir, Henry Holland, and the others were dotted about, each being securely tended by some devoted follower of York. I, my father's eldest son, must show the way of dignity and knightly control, for I was the heir of York and would always be the most closely observed of the family by dint of my status.

Later, news was brought us of Rouen's fall. Somerset's brother, Edmund, having behaved with the witless hysteria of a moonstruck imbecile, surrendering to the French when he had adequate forces to fight them off, and no necessity to submit. With Rouen went Lillebonne, Honfleur, Caudebec, Arques, Dieppe, and Lord Talbot, England's hero-knight, as hostage. Suffolk's reaction was to drag together an army of some six thousand men, place at their head Sir Thomas Kyriel, and despatch them to the battle front. It was in vain. Cowardly, squirming Somerset wrote to King Henry telling him of Suffolk's appalling battle tactics—that he had departed Normandy minus stores, weapons and reinforcements—Parliament leaping at this chance to attack Suffolk. The Queen's pampered pet was accused of having sold England to the King of France and Queen Margaret's father; of preparing his castle for the French when they arrived in England to commandeer the country while he placed his own son upon the Throne in Henry's place. Great and high treason indeed!

Tearfully my French nurse, Anne de Caux, spoke of our land being overrun by enemies who would murder her little pets (these pets being myself and my family) and I think she had long forgotten she too was French—from the Pays de Caux—for she loved us so dearly she had taken our nationality upon herself. Again I was the comforter, smiling as sunnily as I was able, clucking my tongue and telling her God would protect us—aided by my father.

"But the Duke is in Ireland! How can he know what happens here?" she wept. "How can he see the danger we are in and come to our aid in time?"

I confess I frowned at that point. Yet recalling all I remembered of my father I could not recall one time when he did not know all that was going on around him, from smallest occurrence to the mightiest eruption, and I reminded Anne of this, at which she wiped her tears. "I should not doubt. Yet—all the same—he *is* in Ireland."

I sighed, as if impatient of women's ignorance and weakness. "He will hear and he will come should he be needed," I said sternly, convincing myself my words were true. In those days, I saw my father as a King Arthur reborn, it being said of Arthur he would return when England needed him most. So would my father return, I believed, and indeed he did return in 1450—only months after Rouen fell. But more of that later.

The Vixen, as could be expected, was greatly unwilling to allow her precious Suffolk to be impeached for his errors and, remembering the success of Gloucester's fall, she summoned Parliament to Leicester. But now my father acted, fully informed and alert as I had known he would be. Before her ministers could crawl to their seats, slug-like and subservient to the Vixen, the Lord Chancellor was murdered and Parliament scuttled back to its holes like a bevy of terrified rats. Suffolk had no recourse but to appear at the Bar in London, where he soon saw there was to be no mercy allotted him. All except Margaret were against him, for Yorkists desired to free the way for my father, and Somerset's minions to rid themselves of all blame. The Vixen, quaking with fear, saw that Parliament's verdict would be death and hastily had her precious pet banished for five years before sentence could be drawn upon him. But enemies were lurking in wait for him as he fled London, and he escaped only after furious battle when many of his bodyguards and their attackers were slain or maimed. Reaching Ipswich, Suffolk heard that Sir Thomas Kyriel had recaptured Valogne and was now marching to join with Somerset, the Count of Clermont's army in pursuit of him, and Richemont's ahead. On 15th April, 1450, the trio clashed at Formigny, and defeat was most tragically suffered by we English. Four thousand dead! For 150 years—since Bannockburn—we had never suffered defeat in a pitched battle, and now four thousand were slain brutally, and England was no longer the mighty victor she had been in Harry of Agincourt's splendid day.

When I heard of the tragedy, I prayed until my knees ached, and my prayers were for the return of King Arthur with Excalibur brandished in his strong fist, and in my mind's eye I saw him bearing down upon the wretched French, and in my vision King Arthur's face was that of my father. . . .

Whilst I prayed for the Legend-King to rise again, Suffolk took it upon himself to coil into a ball and die like a wounded snake. England had been leeched at Formigny, and he could not survive it. Having written a letter to his son, he summoned his minions together and declared himself innocent of the charges against him, then set sail for France to die in battle like a Viking Lord. But Somerset was panting for his blood, his ship apprehending Suffolk's. It was the *Nicholas of the Tower*, and Somerset was its Captain. At gun point, Suffolk crawled aboard the *Nicholas*, and was greeted with "Welcome, traitor". Shortly, he was being tried, crudely and hastily, by the hating, half-drunken mob aboard the *Nicholas*, and every one of the charges ever brought against him was resurrected, with a new charge to be added: that he had fled England to join the ranks of the King of France. Silently, the favourite watched and, if the sailors desired wails or whimpers they did not receive them. Sullen Suffolk was accused and sentenced to death by beheading, in deference to his rank.

May 1st, 1450, greeted the condemned Duke and saw him curve his greying head onto the block. The sword selected for the execution was blunt and rusty, and it took some half dozen hefty whacks of the blade to decapitate the head, which eventually rolled from the ageing body of the favourite in a flurry of blood and shreds of gore-smeared flesh.

The Vixen, we heard, was inconsolable. Her champions

were being torn from her one by one, and with them her strength and power. Whatever Suffolk had been to her, lover, substitute-father, champion, power-grabber, he was gone now, and she was alone. But knowing the Vixen and her immoral ways, she would not be long in garnering another doting lover. . . .

I wanted to discuss it all; the battles and the execution of the hated Duke; the wailing Vixen in her Palace; the truth concerning her relationship with Suffolk (for, being much a boy of my time and a son of York, I was precocious to a *haute* degree!) but my tutor Croft, grim and snarling, would allow none of my talk. When I would question my nurse, or others, he would appear glum-faced and frowning, to apprehend the answers before they assailed my ears. By all the Saints I despised him, and balked rudely beneath his unwelcome thrall, repulsing his attempts to instruct me. When lessons—a bitter, galling battle—were done for the day I would flounce out to do what pleased me most: don my miniature suit of armour, collect my miniature sword and shield and practise doing battle with my pent-up frustrations to motivate me.

Yet, despite Croft's efforts to keep my mind clean as a sword's blade, some of the truth leaked through, rumour and distortion swelling it. (And perhaps there is no greater distortion given to any words than those passed from mouth to mouth, yet we must make do with this method of newsmongering for it is all we have.) I learnt that after three days of grief and self-imposed starvation, the beautiful daughter of René of Anjou rose from her couch with the spirit and face and mind of a Valkyrie, the determination and ruthlessness of a Queen of Amazons and the rapacity and greed of a ravening wolf, and my thoughts harked back to Isabella de Valois, wife to Edward Second, who had reached our shores as Isabella the Fair, a beauteous maiden and had, by ill usage and twist of fortune become Isabella the She-Wolf. She had shown promise and been lauded and beloved, and yet had become avaricious and malicious, assisted by my ancestor-King's perfidy and perversion. He, a strange sovereign who delighted in digging furrows and toiling on the earth like a bondsman, was as un-Kingly in his fashion as Henry VI, and both married Vixen wives who took lovers to their beds and plotted insurrection in our country. So many French Princesses have wed English Kings and brought the taints and malhumours and witchbrews of the French Royal Line into the English one to deform and blight it. Henry Six's mother had a mad father, from which source he inherited his moonfever, and Isabella the She-Wolf inherited her own father's* ruthlessness and avarice; Margaret the Vixen-Queen brought to us sensuality, lust and the extravagance of her father of Anjou along with his love of warmongering.

'*The Martian Queen is in the ascendant*,' my father wrote in one of his letters to me from Ireland. '*They say her former malice is as naught to what she flaunts now. Others breathe England's air and thrive upon it, but she inhales hatred and feeds off venom and her beauty is the brittle veneer of an Eve. And husband Henry has taken the proffered apple from her palm and gobbled it. . . .*'

Small though I was in years (but not in height) his allusions were not lost upon me. I understood what he meant and my skin shivered as my mind's eye saw the Margaret-Eve proferring the scarlet and lime apple to the witless whining King of England, Satan's vileness lurking behind her mask-like beauty, the coils of her jetty hair being the coils of serpentine tails. A Medusa was Queen of England, and all who looked upon her were doomed. . . . Not for the first time, my spirit writhed unpleasantly in contemplation of such evil ruling our beloved England, and I yearned for my vigorous and determined father to return to London and smite off the Medusa's head as Perseus had done in the ancient legend. On one fact at least I was allowed to question my tutor, Curt Croft as I had named him, and that fact concerned my father's right to the Throne of England. Edward Third (son of Isabella the She-Wolf) had sired many sons and they had been a mettlesome, healthy brood, each in his maturity siring his own brood. It was from Edward's third son, John of Gaunt, by his marriage to Blanche of Lancaster, that the present King derived his claim to the Crown. But my father could claim descendancy twice over from Edward III, through Edward's fifth son, Edmund Duke of York, and through his own mother, Anne Mortimer, who was des-

* Philippe IV, called le Bel.

cended from Lionel, Duke of Clarence, *second* son of Edward Third. So my father was not only sole heir to the dynasty of York but also had a prior claim to the English Throne! Yet Henry VI sat upon that Throne by virtue of his grandfather's having usurped it many years before. (God had punished Henry Fourth for snatching the Crown—he had died a leper.) The fact that my father should have been King burned like a firebrand in my brain, yet there were many, I knew, who pondered and muttered upon his right to rule, for he had gained his descent from Edward Third through women, and there was doubt whether such inheritance was superior or even equivalent to that through males. (Except for Henry Second, who had inherited the Throne through his mother the Empress Matilda, no other King had gained it this way. And, at that time, there had been but one rival claimant, Stephen, and his right had fallen to *him* via a woman.) So my father's claim was drowned in the doubts and theorising of our times, and a mad King reigned, a gawky, pallid puppet whose strings were manipulated by the Vixen. True, Henry Fourth and Fifth and Sixth had ruled for three generations before my father's uncle Edmund of March had died and passed the inheritance to my father, but why should that preclude my father's right? I, with all the bloodlust and straight thinking of the young boy saw no reason why my father should not demand his Crown *now.* I said so many times to Curt Croft until he was nauseous of hearing me repeat the words and snapped that I would do more good unto myself if I memorised my lessons as immaculately as I had memorised my father's ancestry. At the time I thought him a vile fellow, and disloyal to my House, and further shirked my lessons, thinking to spite him when of course I was doing none but myself the harm.

Writing to my father to complain of Croft and beg him to return to London and demand his rights, became one of my regular pastimes. However, my father never showed by word or deed that he upheld the views I aired regarding my tutor and much later I came to realise how unfair I had been to the man who had such evil struggles with the rebellious young heir to York.

By the time Jack Cade's name was bruited about from lip

to lip, with news of his insurrection (he claiming to be the long-dead Edmund Mortimer, brother to my father's mother, Anne) I had all but relinquished hope of my parent breaking from his Irish exile to take London by force.

the gasps and whimpers she would emit at the feel of him within her. Men who raped and ravished were fools, he believed. They would never know the adulation radiated in such abundance by women who were well-loved and well-laid. Some, whom he had bedded years ago, still sought him should he return to their land; one or two had followed him for miles begging for his love-making. To those, and others, he had given freely and with compassion. And now he was in Ireland, having fought in the French Wars and attempted a little of almost every honorable task, and on the morrow he was to have an audience with Richard Duke of York, the Governor of Ireland, upon a matter which was, as yet, totally secret to him.

The girl, Imelda, was growing eager for his body, and again she tried to mount him, this time succeeding. A swatch of her serpentine hair whisked across his face as she moved, at first slowly and then with gathering speed. His eyes upon her heavy, swaying breasts, Jack Cade forgot the Duke of York had ever existed....

Cade, who had battled and fought in ditches, fields, in meadows and ravines, sleeping in mud, swamp, on hay and in farmyard, had never been inside a castle before. The Duke of York's home when Lieutenant of Ireland was a great grey castle in Dublin. Here in 1449, was born his sixth son, George, the future Duke of Clarence; and his fifth son, John, who had died in infancy, had been born in 1448 in Neath. Whatever Cade had expected, he was surprised when he was shown into the Duke's presence. The chamber was small and a generous fire crackled in the grate; arras depicting scenes from the Annunciation and the Fall concealed the great wall stones. In a chair fashioned in the Roman style, carved and gilded, sat the Duke of York, heir to the English Throne. On seeing Cade ushered in, the Duke rose, and it was then the soldier-adventurer experienced surprise, for the Duke was small and plump—just five feet six—and he had expected him to be hugely tall and willow-thin as fighting men usually are, and as he himself was. The Duke was not handsome, but his face was pleasant if a little pudgy, and the smile which dominated his expression was one of sincerity.

Cade fell to one knee before the Duke, at which he was

told to rise and be seated on the stool next the Duke's chair. And then came a rustling from the darker corner of the chamber, and a tall aristocratic woman swept forward to stare hard into Cade's upturned face. She was extremely captivating: elegant, composed, fair, far taller than the Duke, her patrician features commanding instant respect.

"Her Grace, Cecily, Duchess of York," said the Duke, and there was rapt adoration on his own face as he looked at his wife's.

Cade leapt to his feet and bowed again, more humbly, noting the Duchess's feet as he did so. They were far smaller than he would have expected in a woman of her height and, before he had raised himself to his full height, he was considering how she would behave in bed with him—which was always his first thought about a woman, gypsy or duchess. Yet, when he faced Cecily there was no lust glittering in his eyes. One day, this woman might be Queen of England. For that reason alone, he chose not to offend her.

Cecily left almost immediately, her husband following her to the door like a devoted pup, taking her hand and kissing it before she departed. Cade pondered upon the fact that submissive men were always attracted to dominant women, and this woman, whom they called 'Proud Cis' was indeed the proudest he had ever seen. As she allowed her husband to kiss her hand, her manner was that of a Queen receiving gifts from an ambassador. Yet there was love welling in her bright eyes for all that she flaunted such pride. Calculating swiftly in his head, Cade realised that the lovely and slender Duchess had already borne no less than nine children to her Lord, the last boy, George, being only a few months old and yet she was but a few years past thirty and had that glimmer about her skin which he always associated with maidens. Should the daft King in England die childless (which seemed quite likely) this woman would make an enchanting if somewhat haughty Queen. He could not imagine the diminutive Duke in ermine and crimson, assuming the airs of a King, yet Richard Duke of York, descendant of the very first Duke of York, would sit upon the Throne one day, of that he had no doubt. The Duke was returning to his seat now, his cheeks somewhat roseate. It seemed to Cade that he had to collect himself with some effort before he could speak coolly.

"It is fortuitous that we should meet at this vital moment in history," the Duke said, staring deeply into the adventurer's eyes. Cade was puzzled; had the Duke himself not summoned him to this meeting? Why then did he talk as if it were an accidental one? He was soon to know.

"You have been a soldier, and an artisan; you have travelled widely?" Cade nodded. "You fought valiantly in the Wars with France?" This time he did not assent; to do so would have been vanity; however, the Duke did not wait for his reply. "I have heard much of you, Jack Cade, in the past months, and it seems to me you are what I am seeking. You have an able wit—you dearly cherish a gamble, an adventure? In fact, you are like many men of our times, but perhaps just a little more so?"

Cade's appealing grin flashed out.

"I could have found other men with habits similar to yours, but they would not have possessed the extra qualities which are vital to my plan."

"And those are?"

"Your height, Jack Cade, and your colouring. My mother had a brother, Edmund Mortimer, Earl of March, son of Roger Mortimer, Earl of March. Edmund died in 1424, and his rights to the title passed to me, through his sister Anne, my mother. Had he lived, I would not be Earl of March now. Two fortunate accidents brought me my titles, Jack Cade. Edward, Duke of Aumerle and York died at Agincourt, leaving no children. His younger brother gained the title, and that younger brother was my father, the Earl of Cambridge, from whom I received the title after his death. And Edmund Mortimer died childless in 1424. There is only one barricade against loss—of titles, of honour, of inheritance—and that is children. One's own sons to inherit."

Cade, who had none of which he knew, nodded in agreement, wishing the Duke would come to the point.

"England is gripped at its white throat by the Vixen-Queen and her avaricious minions. She is squeezing that throat with all the bloodlust and vituperativeness of which she, Margaret of Anjou, is capable."

"They say she is born under the Sign of Mars, like the

vile Marèchal, Gilles de Rais, who fought with crazed Joan, the Soldier-Maid."

"Aye. And the Sign of Mars brings war and destruction, conflict and hatred. There is a murderer inside everyone born under Mars; some vanquish the murderer; others allow him freedom of their souls and hearts. She—the Vixen—is totally ruled by her soul's evil. Before she came to England, King Henry was a gentle lad, religious and deeply pious. Now he has lost his soul and his eyes gaze from his body like dry ditches. I believe the Vixen has *stolen* the King's soul for Satan, whom she worships."

"I do not doubt it," Cade replied, for he had seen the King some months before, riding through the city streets in London, a vacuous, almost stupefied expression on his thin and mournful face.

"How can a King reign in God's eyes when his soul is in the Devil's possession? That is what I ask myself time and again. It is not meet that a Frenchwoman should destroy our King, and then rule in his stead! One day soon she will usher in all the French hordes to take over our land."

Cade's eyes were wide. He knew what the commonfolk said, that the King was a saint who should have become a monk and not a sovereign. Yet there were always those who would shout them down, saying, "Remember his mad grandsire of France. He suffered like our King suffers now, and he was moonfevered, there's no doubt on it!" But puzzlement was swelling amongst the people, for each dawn brought with it fresh blood, fresh atrocity, fresh pain, and surely a Saint-King's reign should be a peaceful, fruitious time? Yet everywhere men looked, they saw the hand of the Vixen-Queen, her malice and evil enamelled by her blatant beauty—as Eve's had been. It had needed only a few sentences from the Duke of York, England's heir, to settle the criss-cross of confused thoughts which tangled in Cade's head concerning Henry the King. He who had done vigorous battle against the French, hating their greed and rapacity, seeing his companions-in-arms mercilessly slain or deformed by brutally-wielded weapons, now heard the Duke's last words ringing alarmingly in his head: "One day, she will usher in the French hordes to take over our land."

The Duke continued. "I see I have disturbed you, Cade.

But have I convinced you of the danger of the French Vixen?"

"Aye, My Lord, you have, and rightly so!"

"But what of the commonfolk who are not as intelligent or as decisive as we are?" The Duke scrutinised the adventurer, watching for signs of preening at his having included the soldier with himself. There were none, and that was good. For his plan there must be no foolhardiness caused by brash arrogance.

"Who will convince them of the mortal danger in which they languish?" Richard asked.

"Any man who spoke publicly against the King and Queen would have been accused of treason, and mayhap would forfeit his life."

"Assuredly. And that is why I have asked you to visit me, Cade."

The Duke rose and strolled round his room for a moment or two, apparently eyeing a portrait, then examining a worn patch in a tapestry above the hearth.

"There is one positive way of testing the true climate of England, My Lord Mortimer."

Cade jerked up his head. "You called me Mortimer, My Lord?"

"Aye. That is the role you will adopt when you advance into England with your troops to take the Throne in the name of my mother's brother."

There was absolute silence in the room, as Duke and soldier contemplated one another. Then Cade spoke, his voice hoarse.

"I, an Earl? I, become King of England . . .? How can this be—how can I adopt such a deceit? I have no Lordly training; no regal bearing; no knowledge of the ways of Lords and Dukes!" Cade made as if to rise, pondering upon the fact that Richard of York surely had lost his mind when he was exiled from his homeland? A tragic fate for the heir to the Throne.

However, Richard had no intention of allowing his prey to escape back to his hitherto variegated existence. "Stay, My Lord Mortimer!" he commanded. "You love England? You have fought to extrude the French from power there? Now I give you opportunity to extrude them finally and for ever!

Hear, this is my plan. Affecting to be my uncle of Mortimer, risen from the grave—" he smiled, something between a smirk and a grin—"you take the men I shall give you, gathering more followers as you travel London-bound. At each stage of the journey—and during it—you will make it well and fully known that you are the rightful King, being descended from an older brother of Edward Third whilst Henry is descendant of a younger brother. By the time you reach London you will possess a formidable army which will be totally devoted to your cause. Then we shall know London's mood and, I do not doubt it, they will rally to your standard and your Crown, and you shall shortly be King."

"But I am an impostor, My Lord! How can I with all easy conscience sit upon England's Throne and disport myself as its Royal ruler? I know nothing of your uncle—surely I would blunder into mistakes and dilemmas concerning his early life if naught else?"

"There is good reason why men have presumed you dead all these years, My Lord. You lost your memory and wandered abroad—finally reaching Ireland where my wife saw you amongst a company of soldiers and recognised you from the portrait of Mortimer which hangs above our bed. Now you have been informed of your true identity *but* there is excellent cause for your failing to remember details of your youth. . . .

"Come," Richard ordered, and Cade silently followed him from the living-chamber beyond into a larger room hung with violet and ivory tapestries, its centrepiece a broad and stately bed clothed with violet silk and adorned with sable rugs. Footstools and benches created by master carpenters lined the walls, and there were many portraits between the tapestries—paintings of the Duke's and Duchess's ancestors. Above the bed hung an enormous, wieldy frame which clasped the portrait of a young and comely man. At sight of it, Cade could not help but gasp out loud. The man flaunted the composure of a Lord, and there were gems upon his long fingers and a collar of gold and emeralds about his throat, but it was his face which astonished Cade, for the man—Edmund Mortimer—(who would have been heir to the Throne had he not died) was his double.

Richard of York was smiling smugly as he looked from the

portrait to the adventurer and back again. "Did I not tell you there was none other as suitable as you, My Lord? For the commonfolk—who would not recognise my uncle if he stepped in front of them—there is no need of such a likeness, but concerning the nobles who surround the King—especially the older ones—there must be no doubt in their minds that you are Edmund Mortimer and everything the King is not: handsome, tall, valiant, dashing, and articulate."

"If I do not lend myself to this plot, then England will be aswarm with French . . ." Cade voiced his thoughts musingly.

"And there is every possibility that the Vixen will whelp a Frenchman's brat and plant it upon the Throne when Henry dies, or, perhaps even before. . . ."

The Duke's words stabbed into Cade's mind like burning tapers and he paled, his fingers clenching and unclenching. "Think you she would stoop so low?"

"Did she not take Suffolk to her bed frequently—and others, too—and ever without shame or repentance?"

"Aye, I have heard it thus." Cade's mind was reeling back into the past. He, fighting beside English companions-in-arms against the avaricious French, had seen the slaughter of the Marling family in the village where they battled. Other families were slain, too, for the French temporarily overpowered the English, pillaging and murdering until English reinforcements galloped up, their swords reflecting the sunlight. The village had been composed of English families who had journeyed to France along with the Duke of York some time before, remaining behind when he departed for they had fruitful little farms and vineyards now. The Marlings had fed Cade and his companions for over a week and that had been sufficient time for the adventurer to woo Molly Marling (passionately, as was his nature) and to bed with her. A strange girl she, not beautiful, yet having a mobile and fascinating face which glowed when she smiled, and never dulled even when she was in quiet mood. One week, and Cade had seen beyond his facile and vacuous existence into the future which he had hitherto scorned. What he saw was Molly Marling bending at the hearth smiling, his children playing about the floor, the youngest tugging at her skirt eager for her attention, and himself walking in the door, to receive the smile which elevated his spirits and fed his dreams. Whether he would have reached the stage of asking Molly's hand in marriage he did not know for, when the battle was over, he found her body flung over a fence like a moppet's from which the stuffing had been wrenched by a vicious child. There was a gash in her throat, her skirt was burnt, and her legs charred, and between her shoulders protruded the hilt of a French dagger. Behind her lay her home, a smoking ruin, and dotted about were the slain cattle which had so delighted her father when they were thriving on his land.

First, Cade had known a fury so intense that the pressure of it had swelled inside his head to a point almost beyond pain, then had come the compassion and the misery, to be followed in later days by such an acute loneliness he had almost forsworn the desire to live. A young girl, innocent, gay, appealing, hacked and gouged like a quintain in the lists, and flung across her father's fence as if she were little but an old sack.

This was the French way now: crude, bestial, arrogant, and their companions the Burgundians and the Armagnacs were no better. Hawks and vultures, savage boars, leopards sprung to life from the French standard with claws rapacious and sharp . . . not men but beasts, all honour and humanity hacked from them, swamped by greed and goldlust, by base passions swarming within them like bees avid for pollen. And Margaret of Anjou was niece of the King of France. . . . Her son would be his great-nephew, and half-French *if* his father were King Henry. If he were not, then Satan only knew who his sire would be: an Armagnac? a Burgundian? one of the French King's men? A shudder coursed over his flesh. England a suburb of France. . . . Mentally, he reviewed the incredible military successes of Henry V. When the Lion of Agincourt had died in 1422, he had been recognised as King of France in Normandy, Picardy, Maine, Champagne, Burgundy, Flanders, Guienne, and much of Gascony, and the Burgundians and the Flemish had been loyal allies of the English. Not since Henry II had so much of France been possessed by England. By 1428, all of Gascony and Guienne had been lost, and now the Flemish-Burgundian dominions were stretching towards Nevers, Charolais, and the Franche Comté, as well as Burgundy,

Luxembourg, Picardy, Flanders, Brabant and Liège. And the French had snatched Upper and Lower Normandy, Valogne, Verneuil, and Pont de l'Arche, Evreux, Lisieux, Gournay, Rouen, Mantes and the cowardly Somerset had *given* them Honfleur, Lillebonne, Dieppe, Arques, Caudebec. . . . The 15th of April, 1450, had seen the French and English clash at Formigny, where four thousand English were slain (Henry V had needed only twenty-four thousand to conquer France!). It was the end for English suzerainty in France, and the beginning of the Rule of the Leopards in that country. Now, the English owned little more than the tiny pebble which was Calais. . . .

Once, Henry V had been the victor, but now it was the turn for France. A strong King in London would have fought back the steady and insidious advance of the French and their allies, and kept his Queen safe beneath his palm where she could not brew her evils and cause damage to his land. Instead, waffle-headed Henry VI wore the Crown (as crookedly as a jester wore his cap, so some people said) and the King of France's rapacious niece Margaret ruled England, Ireland and Calais, and had plans to invite her countrymen into her husband's domain. . . . Indeed, perhaps the recent great losses in France had all been cunningly planned by the Vixen and were not the gross yet undesigned misfortune which they appeared at first. Whatever other faults Jack Cade possessed, lack of patriotism was not amongst them. A bastard, he had made his country his sire, and now he saw it threatened by the murderers of Molly Marling and thousands of others of his kinsmen.

Turning his dark eyes upon the heir to the English throne, he said, "What would you have me do?"

It seemed that the Duke had been holding his breath until this moment, for now it hissed from between his teeth like a stream of gas escaping from burning coal.

"My Lady Wife has arrangements in process for your schooling as an Earl . . . yet I see there will be little need, for your composure is knightly, your mien admirable."

"Did you expect me to be brash and uncouth, My Lord?" Cade's lips curved into a smile but his eyes were cold.

The Duke, who had never possessed much tact, fingered

the tassel on his sleeve, and said : "Soldiers—especially mercenaries—are rarely elegant charmers."

"What does her Grace plan for my transformation?"

"Er—new clothes, I presume, and gems—and a jewelled sword. And of course you will be given details of our plans to place you on the Throne."

"Her Grace is partner to this scheme?"

"Indeed. It was her idea. She is an exceptional woman, intelligent, shrewd, farsighted. When you have won the Crown, she will tell you what you must do next, and ever after. You have realised, of course, that you will be but a token King—a figurehead behind which I and my Lady Wife shall rule England? There can be no question of your assuming *any* degree of power whatsoever—at *any* time." Richard attempted to look stern, but failed. He was wishing heartily that this interview would end so that his adored and competent Cecily might take charge.

A picture flashed through Cade's mind : the charred and mutilated body of Molly tossed brutally atop the fence where she had leaned the previous night to be kissed by him. . . . Abrupt though the Duke's demands had been, he had no doubt of his intention—or of his part in the plan.

Smiling, he replied, "Of course, My Lord Duke."

It was many weeks later, as the Sheriff of Kent raised his sword to plunge it in his heart that Cade knew he had been more than a token King. He was a chosen victim . . . one of the litany of substitute victims who voluntarily gave or were forced to give their lives in place of their King or master. From the first, Richard of York had been aware his scheme would end with Cade's death; never for one moment had he believed the soldier-adventurer would become a King, puppet or otherwise.

They made their headquarters in Kent, Cade and his gaggle of followers, from there despatching incendiary proclamations carefully planned to incite the country into direct revolt against the Vixen-Queen.

The main theme of the proclamations was that the enraged and malicious Queen intended to take her vengeance upon the people for the death of her *amour*, Suffolk. She was planning, so Cade declared publicly, to ruin England with fire and sword, leaving it a battered wasteland where no man might make his living. There were many eager to listen to scandal against the Queen, and many more when the accusatory words poured from the lips of a grandson of their great hero, Edward Third. Cade-Mortimer had little trouble swaying those who heard him towards the cause of Edward Third's descendant, who promised he would banish the miscreants from their *haute* positions, drag down the avenging Queen from her begemmed Throne, he himself reigning in her place along with the Duke of York, his nephew. Those who had more knowledge of Mortimer's death two decades before spoke little of their doubts concerning the true identity of the rebel leader for the good of their country was uppermost in their minds, and the rebel leader's face radiated honesty and sincerity—qualities which the people had not seen for many a day, and for which they hungered. And, after a while, Cade truly began to believe what he told his audiences : that he was Mortimer; that he and York were what England desperately needed; that the Vixen-Queen fully intended to desecrate their country. He forgot how grief for Molly had first spurred him, and now was conscious only of a task he must fulfil, or else disappoint the people—and himself.

No less than twenty thousand men of every variety and shape rallied to the cry of Mortimer : peasants and farmers, soldiers and itinerants, mercenaries eager for loot, criminals and gypsies, minstrels and strolling players, their ranks edged with heralds from the Dukes of Norfolk and Exeter, York's devoted allies, whose brilliant costumes lent authenticity to the rabble.

Through towns and villages and hamlets the army marched, its ranks swelling at every stop and, at their head, bold and triumphant rode Cade-Mortimer, resolute, inspired, determined. And in his mind's eye before him, glittering provocatively, he was ever conscious of a Crown, jewelled and spired, and the gnarled yet slender prelate's hands which clasped it in preparation for his own coronation.

Already I hear the people call me Shrew and Witch and Vixen, yet I am mere woman, and a creature of Anjou, pleasure-loving, sensual and often arrogant and I am still so young yet I must bear the weight of being King and Queen of England when I long to dance and romp and sing—and bed with a true husband. For poor weak, addled Harry Six is no true husband! Astonishingly, despite his lack, I cannot blame him though I yearn for a husband to fold me in his wide arms and crush me to him, driving the blood from my lips with his kisses. . . . Unfortunate creature of Anjou I, who has no lusty mate to satiate her lusts. . . . Yet what can I do? *What*? If I weep, there will be outcries at my weakness. If I rage they will call me Shrew (which indeed they do already); and if I lean upon some stalwart man, there will be viper-tales about my taking him to my bed. And *that* I swear I have never done, not with any of the men linked scandalously with my name. Tears start when I think of poor and faithful Suffolk, who was as a father to me. Vilely was he slain, hacked and brutalised, and *he did not deserve it*! Had my husband been a man of might and goodly with a sword, he could have prevented Suffolk's death; but he is weakly as a reed tossed and smitten by the wind, and daily his mind droops and hollows. What *can* I do?

If Henry could only bed with me—be stirred by my body and my face and implant the Royal seed within me, then would the Throne be secured, and sons be born! This strange moonfever he displays does not strike at every generation; some are born whole and vigorous betwixt the mad ones. Weak Harry's mother brought the evil seed to England, straight from her father, who was thus fevered, and her mother was a debauched harlot, yet she herself, Catherine de Valois, was untainted. I vow I could bear a comely and healthy heir for England, and then would the tattle cease; they would not abominate me if I were mother to the heir! The English are ever tender to the bearers of their Kings. No doubt they curse me as barren and having cost them dear with their lands in France, yet if I could bear them a son, they would forgive me and take me to their hearts. I am not all steel and bone! I crave love like all women! Yet Harry has none to give me, for what love he manufactures is preserved for his Saints and his God. Sometimes, if I ponder upon this fact hysteria bubbles in my throat and breast and my hands claw like an old dame's. For full length of life I am bound by God's law to an impotent and sickly King who cannot give me sons, and the brunt of England's hatred is directed against me—not against *him*, for many call him Saint. *I* am the scapegoat for their enmities, their discontents.

Who would be woman in this tempestuous and troubled age, when being man is vile enough? Men can fight and rage, whore and cheat, and none will gainsay them for 'tis believed to be man's right to behave thus. And man is not expected, above else, to bear and deliver children, his reputation sullied should he prove barren through no fault of his own! God asks too much of woman! Has He no pity, no insight? All pleasure is the man's, the consequences to be borne—literally—by woman. Mother Nature is never barren; each spring the burgeoning buds swell and ripen and flutter open and there is never winter's infertility in full bright summer. Yet I am in my summer now—hardly past my springtime—and I am barren as though advancing into dotage. And all around me are schemers and plotters; men eager to do me harm—men ravening to slay my poor pudding-witted Harry! I cannot turn but enemies spring up and allies are wickedly put down! If only I had an heir in my arms! A fair and bonny boy bred of England's stalwart spirit and Anjou's sunny pleasaunces....

Oh God, worker of miracles, see my great need and work a miracle for me! Fill my womb with a son for England! A fair and living son, bright witted and comely!

DEATH OF A PUPPET PRINCE, 1450

The Duke of York, aided by his shrewd wife, had planned for every possible occurrence on Cade's inroad into England. The words which spilled from Cade's lips were those of Proud Cis and ambitious Richard, telling the soldier-adventurer's gullible audiences that the Duke of York would be brought back into England's favour to his rightful place beside the King—if Mortimer's rebellion were successful. Too, there would be the abolition of taxes and all corruption would be halted at high levels; those lawyers who worked for the rich against the poor would be smartly dealt with; and the crippling Ordinance of Labourers—that which prevented men from labouring where they could find the most satisfying wage—would be discarded.

Now the joyous Cade had a new name, given him by the gullible, believing hordes, and that name was John Amend-All and, as he rode victory-bound to London, his own selected standard fluttered near by him: the White Wolf, eyes gimlet-bright, teeth sharp, preparing to rip out the throats of corruption and trickery, June's heat bathing the thousands of marchers who accompanied that banner in a haze of wit-dulling, mesmeric light. In London, Marguerite of Anjou heard of their proximity with shivers of horror. She had asked God for an heir to the Kingdom, and He had sent her Mortimer in full battle array, accompanied by thousands of supporters!

The Staffords, William and Humphrey, the Duke of Buckingham's cousins, were selected to deal with the advancing contingent of rebels, and they set out accompanied by a force which was more like a vanguard by comparison to Cade-Mortimer's hordes, no one having truly assessed the size of the rebel army.

Blackheath was chosen by Cade for his camp, and there he set up his headquarters at the White Hart Inn, Southwark, where many came to pay court to the new 'King' whilst Cade discussed the actual capitulation of the city with London's Lord Mayor, Thomas Charlton. Great was his optimism now; London steamed in the June heat before him, rich, indolent, promising, and within its walls lay the Throne and Crown, the Crown Jewels, the ermine, and the Abbey where he would shortly be crowned King of England. Molly was long forgotten now, and with her the motives which had set him on his journey to England's capital, for greater men than Cade had been corrupted by far less.

News of the Staffords' army, reaching Cade, ensured that his camp at Blackheath was deserted rapidly, he and his men scampering into Kent. However, this was by no means a retreat but a carefully-laid plan to avoid being besieged within the hastily-constructed stockade which Cade's followers had erected around their bivouac. The freedom of Kent would provide all that Cade required for his scheme to repulse the Staffords and—they now heard—the King himself, he galloping eagerly but ignorantly behind William and Humphrey.

This picture of the King as upright foe, anxious to protect his Kingdom, was not one which consorted well with the picture Cade had painted for his men of the bumbling, semi-stupefied monarch gripped in his most vulnerable place by the rapacious Vixen-Queen. However, contact with the Royal army revealed not a gallant and competent monarch leading his men, but a confused and shaken King, cheeks sunken, eyes hollow; a man who leapt almost from the saddle at every sound, every movement. Loud was the laughter from Cade's army as they met head on with that of the King and the two Staffords and, later, when the Royal hordes were slain and the Staffords with them, the King had to be supported upon his horse by two chalk-cheeked and gore-spattered aides as he and his stupefied Queen fled to Kenilworth and sanctuary.

Cade, circumventing the battlefield, observed the slaughtered and maimed bodies, the limbless trunks, the headless shoulders, the ditches swimming with blood, and was gripped by an exhilaration stronger than any which had assailed him before. Not the reek of the fresh blood, metallic and penetrating, nor the great victory caused his elevation of spirit. It was easy, after this swift and complete success to believe he had conquered England itself, and was already inches within the Crown's reach, and this was the reason for his exhilaration, such being its strength that it evaporated the last vestiges of his wisdom and caution. Since he had landed, and called Kent to the standard of the White Wolf, he had been revered and worshipped, men had bowed and knelt before him, women and adoring girls had been eager to lie with him, and he had bedded with every female for whom he had energy. He had always had women eager for his favours, for he was straight and handsome, but now there was the added spice of adulation in their eyes, the lisp of awed femininity when they addressed him.

"Mortimer, you will be a King crowned, before the month is out," he whispered as he gazed down upon a hacked and bloodless body, the sword hand severed from the wrist, the sword still grasped in its palm. And it was then he had the first hallucination, seeing a glittering aureole of gold being offered him in ghostly white hands, an aureole laden with gems which he knew to be the Crown of England. . . . "*Take me! Take me!*" he heard a voice saying, low but urgent, and resolution gripped him afresh.

"Before the month is out!" he said aloud. "Before the month is out!"

Further hallucinations followed, one upon the other, until Cade was unsure as to what was reality and what fantasy. Having taken up his lodgings again at the White Hart he comported himself as a great Prince holding elegant court, and there it was that the Duke of Buckingham and the King's Chancellor, Archbishop Kemp, visited the new conqueror, Mortimer, to enquire of him his next plans.

Cade-Mortimer, like so many lowborns believing arrogance and bumptiousness were signs of high breeding, swilled ale and gobbled pie before the King's men, keeping them waiting an unconscionably long time for his reply. When he spoke, it was to demand an audience with the King himself, it being obvious from his tone that he believed himself far superior to the King and already, in fact, King in all but name and crowning. So, shortly he rode arrogantly into London, no man rising to prevent him, the Mayor giving him official greeting. He wore a goldstudded suit which recently had covered the form of Sir Humphrey Stafford, and which boasted the Stafford knots. The day was the third of July—and hot.

Pausing at Old St Swithin's, Cade-Mortimer raised his sword, clashing it against stone, and bellowed, "Now is Mortimer Lord of this City!"

The execution of Lord Say, High Treasurer, and Cromer, Sheriff of Kent rapidly followed, their heads being displayed in every street amidst raucous screeches, and yells of joy. After this, the bloated Cade having dined at Gristes House, he looted the House stealing and snatching all which could be carried. Breaking and entering came next at Green Gate, home of an Alderman and Sheriff of the city. The new conqueror could not have behaved with less wisdom. Bleeding, ragged heads upon poles, and being guilty of plundering one's host were not conducive to trust and peace of mind and the Londoners—a shrewd people—were quick to see they had supported unwisely. No true Mortimer would have behaved thus, they declared, and others who had thought to see security beneath the rebel's rule saw instead all the evils with which they were only too bitterly familiar.

Other rebels had fallen, even when they had risen against child Kings, as Wat Tyler had done in the reign of Richard Second, yet Cade had absorbed nothing of their strategy, seeing all his movements now as those given him by Divine Right of Kings, forgetting all the mistakes which genuine Kings made despite their Divinity. . . . Having withdrawn with his plunder to Southwark, he was preparing for another ambitious sortie into the city when he discovered its drawbridge securely clamped shut and lookouts patrolling. All he had sought was being withheld from him and a furious anger, choking and devouring, embraced him like an instrument of torture. He was the immature child deprived of its toy; the prospective monarch deprived of his Crown. There could be no solution but head-on battle.

Through the night the struggle raged, men dying outright and men falling to their deaths in the river with little count being kept of them because of the darkness, lanterns and *flambeaux* doing little to ease the gloom. When morning irradiated the sky, the rebels retreated back to Blackheath to lave their wounds, and soon word was brought them of the

King promising he would pardon all those who deserted the rebel leader and went peaceably back to their own homes.

Choking down his bitterness, Cade sought the King's pardon in the name of John Mortimer, preparing to depart with his loot, then learned Jack Cade was still a rebel and traitor, the pseudonym alone having been pardoned. To flee was his only resort, so he made for Kent, bedraggled and wretched, a Puppet Prince with his strings slashed, the sawdust having seeped from his limbs. It was there, after a week's scavenging and begging, that the proud and belligerent soldier-adventurer was slain by the Sheriff of Kent.

Two brief months he had schemed and fought and hoped, and now his straight and slender body—which women had so adored—was hacked into four and impaled on the four gates of London, the head being placed upon a spike on London Bridge itself.

And that was the end of the Puppet Prince, who had swaggered and whored and pillaged, and had failed to learn his actor's part with sufficient thoroughness to comport him towards the successful conclusion of the play which the Duke of York had named "Gauging the Lie of the Land" and Cade himself had called "King Mortimer is Crowned".

EDWARD OF YORK, 1453:
A CHILD IS BORN FOR LANCASTER

My father learned much from Jack Cade's insurrection. He learned that England was not totally against a new claimant to the Throne; that indeed England was not sufficiently united to feel hostility against anything or anyone and be able to put that enmity into action. Even in a small nation there is a vast strength in total unity. Perhaps my father, Richard Duke of York, would be the man to teach England the value of this? I prayed that it would be so.

My father did not write to me of Jack Cade and his plans, so I snatched at smatterings of gossip and carelessly-abandoned words and wove from these a little of the truth. Again, my tutor Croft refused to inform me when I requested details from him, and again I bitterly resented his attitude. (How contrite I would be later when my father told me Croft had been given stern orders by him not to let slip any facts which, by my knowledge of them, could harm me should there be a putative move towards the Duke of York's heir by the Lancastrians. We lived in a violent age, my father had said to my tutor, and should our enemies feel the need they would not hesitate to capture the heir of York, then might follow torture, cruelty, until he spilled all his father's plans and schemes.)

England at this time was a tartan of plot and counterplot, malice, murder, and misery, the Vixen-Queen leaping with shock when she heard the latest news from France: Caen, loyal to my father when he was Regent of France, refused to capitulate to Somerset whom its Captain abhorred, he defending the Royal city in the name of the Duke of York. The wife of Somerset, a trembling, puling creature, acquitted herself as weakly as she had at Rouen, falling upon her knees when a stone crashed dangerously near her and her children, and begging her husband to forgo his attack on Caen. Somerset, who never could resist his spouse's tears, demanded that the Captain of Caen surrender. However, the

Captain refused outright, and it was then that Somerset committed his most cowardly and revolting act.

Charles VII, King of France, was also present at the siege, and his great desire was to reclaim the city for the Crown. The citizens themselves—sick of the brutality and slaughter and longing for the days of the ancient regime, were tricked into opening their gates to the French—and Somerset was the trickster. Gluttonous for revenge against the rebellious Captain, Somerset had allowed the city to fall into French hands when, by more equable a scheme, it could have remained English. Now, not only Caen but Somerset was in French hands, and the French—ever avaricious—were demanding a ransom composed of the Coward-Duke's artillery for his freedom. The artillery—England's hope and support in France—was passed into Charles's hands without a gesture of resistance.

How the Vixen-Queen raged and ranted when she heard this daunting news! And how the English sickened, knowing her minion, Somerset, was responsible for this outrage . . . the loss of Caen and England's artillery to free the blanched and quaking Somerset! Fresh hatred welled against the French Vixen and her menials. *She* was responsible for the appalling loss of all that Great Harry of Agincourt had won for our land. *She* was in league with the French, and had placed Somerset in charge in France knowing of his yellow soul, knowing he could lose all we possessed to Charles. Such was the enmity now that those who had dithered, making excuses for the Queen's youth and the King's monkishness, forthwith rallied to the cause of the Yorkists, backing my father's right to the Crown, for he had proved himself in battle, it being an exceptional man who could command both France and Ireland and be truly loved in both—even by active patriots.

Later, I would hear all from my father's lips. How the loyal Captain of Caen had escaped and fled straight to his Duke in Ireland where he spilled the truth to him: the dishonour, the humiliation, the grief. And my father, gauging the time as right, began massing his army of 4,000, helped by his loyal followers, spirited Warwick, his nephew; Salisbury; Norfolk; Exeter. They wasted no second in marching towards London intent upon routing the foulness resident there.

"We were eager to have justice done!" my father told me later. "To purify England's air; to see that those who had allowed anarchy in France would be brought to heel, and be forced to pay their dues for their ineptitude. When we reached London, we found the city struggling to survive yet drowning in gloom. The loss of our artillery and the gaggle of disasters in France had so impoverished the King and Queen that they could not raise one cannon to blast us from their city! Which was indeed great luck for us, my boy!" Eagerly I nodded. "Instead, they were forced to call Cardinal Kemp to pacify us with words, and he told us—with all the earnestness he could muster gleaming from his eyes—that Parliament would shortly be summoned to impeach the traitor, Somerset. Reluctantly, I believed him. Only time could tell whether his words held truth."

"And what happened then, my Lord Father?"

"Why, the traitor himself pelted into London, launched himself piteously at the Vixen's feet (no doubt he had learned much of such humble behaviour from his wife!) and told her that he was attacked because he was the last great noble able to support the Crown and those who wore it and that his enemies knew this, and were ravenous for his blood. 'But,' he told the Vixen, 'where would she be without his loyalty? The Duke of York, vicious and ambitious, would soon wear the Crown should he, Somerset, be put down.'" My father's eyes twinkled, and I smiled at him trustingly, saying, "And the Vixen believed him?"

"Aye, that she did! Lapped up his lies and his charm and when charges were brought against him, she dismissed them all! It became obvious then that the Frenchwoman had taken him not only into her confidence, but into her bed! Another foolish, lying, cowardly lover to add to her quiver of bed-knaves! If ever a woman chose ill it was she! Pah!" My father uttered a most derogatory sound of disgust.

"But Parliament refused to be swayed?"

"Indeed. When Parliament was summoned and demanded Somerset's impeachment, it was the Tower for the Coward-Duke—whatever his Vixen-lover demanded! And to the

Tower he went, and back went I to Ireland—satisfied that some small part of justice had been effected."

"What did you feel when you learned of the Vixen's next act?"

"The chilliest fury I'd ever felt, my son! She had her meagre and vacillating army summoned, their first move being to release the Coward-Duke! And, before we had finished gasping, she had created him England's Constable!"

I gasped, too. "He would have let in the French! Opened London's gates to Charles, as he had Caen's!"

"That is what we feared and dreaded, Edward. The new Constable was a coward, a weakling, a knave, *and* a cheat. No insult was too strong or to great to be flung at him, and *she* had made him Head of England's armies! Had she planned to make the most disastrous move possible, she could not have done better than this! England flared, yet we had suffered a harsh and debilitating winter and were impoverished from the Wars. For the moment, we could do naught but stay still, yet our sores were festering, we being aware that we had many more on our side then before the traitor became Constable. And now the Vixen made another foolish move: publicly, she announced she was on the side of the Red Rose of Lancaster and naturally it was accepted that the King was a Lancastrian, too. Having taken sides, the King had lost the safety and security which Royal neutrality had yielded him, and the Vixen had caused it."

At that point, a servant brought in haunches of meat, apple jelly and custards and Hippocras, so while we munched my father told me more of the story, I frowning at the lack of wisdom displayed by the Vixen in dismissing her Royal husband's neutrality so carelessly.

"1451 was a gloomy year for England. Wars and skirmishes, battles and losses had brought us naught but poverty and despair. In their Royal palace, even the King and his haughty Queen were facing hunger for the amount of credit which they had assimilated was a mountainous sum, and the tradesmen were hammering their fists upon the King's table itself, demanding their bills be paid. We English were plunged into sombre mood for only recently Charles of France had been as poor as we now were, his army starving and riddled with ills, his every battle lost. It was not easy to accept this *volte face* : we starving, the French now victors and gradually reclaiming our land in France, their coffers being stacked with gold and loot . . . and all of it due to the Vixen!" My father wiped his mouth of beef juice, and drank deeply of Hippocras.

"She—wily whore—pretended to share England's despair, wailing and moaning loud of our losses and poverty .We, knowing her only too bitterly of old, turned our shoulders against her hypocrisy. And, whilst she played her little sham, Charles and his armies snatched Normandy and Aquitaine and showed no signs of ceasing their attacks on our possessions.* Yet, though the people screamed 'Treason! Treason!' at Somerset and his Vixen whore, they both hid behind the shambling, yet gentle figure of Harry Six—still beloved by many, still the only child of Great Harry of Agincourt. And, whilst wastrel and whore were screened by Great Harry's son, they were safe. The King was gaining his martyrdom whilst still on Earth—for each one of the tragedies which struck at our hearts made him all the more pitiful in many eyes—it being because of this that a Yorkist follower was flung into the Tower for suggesting in Parliament that I be made *official* heir to the Throne."

My father coughed, lowering his eyes. He was never one to accept failure easily and, in front of me, his young heir, it was doubly difficult. Seeking to take his mind from this, I proffered the wine jug, and he nodded for me to refill his goblet. When he had drunk, I spoke lightly.

"What happened then, my Lord Father?"

"It grieves me to speak of it to you, my courageous boy, but I rose in revolt against Somerset, and the Vixen, in an attempt to save the King from their evil activities. And then was I most cruelly tricked! Cardinal Kemp despatched a messenger to me, ordering me to give myself up to my King and return to my duties, to which I replied that I had never neglected my duties—nor left them. In proof, I offered to give myself up to the King on the agreement that the traitor Somerset was brought to trial. Returning to King and Cardinal, the messenger gave them my words, returning

* Holinshed wrote: 'In Aquitaine alone the Kingdom was losing three Archbishoprics, thirty four Bishoprics, fifteen counties, one hundred and five Baronies, a thousand *capitaineries*.'

forthwith carrying the King's message: '*Somerset shall be arrested and charged.*'

"Joyfully then I dismissed my army and set out for the King's camp, he having accompanied his army to defend the city. Believing the bloodshed and misery were over, I felt myself ten years younger and a hopeful man. Yet, all the while I was approaching the King, Somerset was gabbling to his Vixen the course of events that day and she was riding swiftly to join the King her husband. So, I had barely reached the King's side when the Vixen threw herself into the tent between us, her eyes seeming to flash fire as she spat words of fury and reproach at her drooping spouse. Had I doubted before then that she totally ruled England, I had proof of it now. Harry Six was a moppet filled with decaying sawdust which seemed to leak from his body even as I watched. His eyes were those of a dog being whipped by a beloved but brutal master, and his hands shook like a scare-bird's flapping in the wind. The day was lost for York and won for Lancaster, for Somerset swiftly followed his Royal whore into the tent and I saw myself tricked and deceived."

I could not conceal the tears in my eyes. So hopeful and joyous a day had been ruined by Satan's Queen, and my father was thus betrayed! I urged him to continue his story.

"Humiliated, I was bound and taken to London where I was forced to take oath that I would never again raise arms against the King my master, after which I was free to return to my home and your mother, who waited in terror lest I be slain in London."

"You swore never to fight the King again, my Lord?"

"Aye, but I had not sworn never to take up arms against the Vixen and her lover!" My father's eyes glinted and I grinned widely.

"A year passed, and France grew in tumult. Aquitaine—so long under English rule—was raising its back against the French, and Bordeaux frowned whilst its trade diminished and its stocks of wine soured, the citizens greeting each English visitor as if he were a god. They found their King Charles intransigent. He had vowed to reclaim his country and he was indifferent to all complaints whilst he battled to do so. The townships which had flourished whilst I was Regent were sick at heart for the English to become their masters again. February, 1453, and we Yorkists were still biding our time, observing and waiting, when the news reached us of the Vixen's pregnancy. . . ." Now my father's cheeks blazed.

"Her . . . pregnancy?" She, wife to Henry the Monk who had taken a vow of chastity, who seemed to court dazedness where other men courted vigour, was with child?

"Yes. And she claimed the child to be of the King's own seed." My father paused as if unable to consume this fact. Even though the Vixen's pregnancy had become part of the fading past, it still irked him. For the Vixen had borne a son, a Prince of Wales who was given the same name as myself: Edward.

An heir for the Lancastrians: a boy who thrived and grew lusty in his cradle; a comely babe, and innocent, yet who had displaced my father as heir-presumptive and drowned the Yorkists' hopes in one move. Edward, Prince of Wales, my namesake, born of a rapacious, whoring mother, and a monkish, impotent father, he displaying such strength of form and *haute* intelligence that it was hard enough to believe him their son even had we believed the King capable of that deed necessary for the procreation of heirs. . . . Which no Yorkist did believe! And in this we were accompanied by no less than the King himself! For, on hearing he had sired a son, Harry the Monk declared bemusedly, "His father must be the Holy Spirit, for it is not I. . . ." We could have taken it for a gay jest had the King's moonfever not increased tenfold in the last few years, he labouring between bouts of mindlessness and ones of confused semi-sanity. Even those who had called him saint were now whispering one word amongst themselves concerning Great Harry's son: madness.

THE SUN IN SPLENDOUR WITH THE ROSE: 1461

Many years have passed since I sat at my father's knee listening to his story of his mistreatment at the hands of the Vixen-Queen. Years which saw the birth of her bastard, Somerset's boy, whom they chose to call Prince of Wales and pretend he was sprung from the Monk-King's seed; years which saw furious battle ensue between our two Houses—York and Lancaster—and the Battle of Northampton, at which I commanded part of our army—and at which we defeated the Monk-King, taking him prisoner; years which saw, only one month after Northampton, the death of my father and younger brother Edmund at the battle of Wakefield. They crowned my father's head with a paper crown and stuck it above the gates of York, and I shall never forget the fury which raged in me at this. Had I been half-hearted in my actions before that day then before the gates of York life and death became hideous reality! I was eighteen, and had fought in battles since I was thirteen, when I left the peace of Ludlow eager to join in the quest for the Crown, yet that previous experience had not prepared me for my father's and brother's deaths. In youth so long separated from my father the Duke, and now his body decapitated and the subject of cruel gibes and taunts! Later, when night fell, it came home to me that I was now the Duke of York and heir-presumptive to the Throne (for who could in all seriousness recognise Somerset's bastard as heir?) and that, if we Yorkists desired to win over the Vixen and her minions, it would have to be I who led them to victory. . . . And when we won, as I was determined we would, I, Edward of York, would be King of England!

King! The knowledge raced along my bones like battle-fever's sweats and chills, numbing my grief and burdening me with an emotion which I later was to identify as fearful anticipation. Anticipation which grew, swarming within me like lust for a woman, making me eager to claim England's Throne as mine.

Soon after my father's tragic death, the second battle of St Albans was fought, the Vixen winning again, yet losing all she had won by allowing her army to loot the abbey and town, thereby giving the citizens of London cause to decide they would prevent her from entering their city. I was at Shrewsbury when I heard, the news being brought me by Warwick, son of Salisbury (a great and ambitious man and supporter of the misled King until that moment when it became obvious he was too bemused and addle-witted to reign alone.) Furious at the Vixen's success at St Albans and eager to avenge my father's and brother's deaths, I rapidly gathered my army and rode to glorious victory at the battle of Mortimer's Cross, after which Warwick and I galloped to London. Here we were greeted joyously, for we were seen as the Londoners' protectors—we being all that lay betwixt them and the Vixen and her bloodgreedy followers. The citizens smiled and cheered at sight of us, Warwick telling me of his plans as we rode through the streets nodding and bowing, in answer to the cheers.

"The Duke your father is dead, and you are now heir to the Throne, My Lord. London will have none of the Vixen, and her spouse is plunged into the shadow world of the imbecile. . . . I see your fate lying clear before me : you must be crowned King and I shall be the instrument which ensures your crowning success. . . ." He glanced at me, his high dark brows arched, his eyes glittering black almonds beneath, whilst my cheeks flooded with colour.

"I, King? I had thought to wait many a month before that time."

"The hour is propitious, My Lord. Times are unruly and opportunity fleeting. Should we allow this hour to pass with its fruits ungathered I vow both we and England shall weep many a galling tear after it."

"You speak truth, Warwick. But what of the King—and what of Edward the Bastard? How may we overlook their claims and not be vilified?"

Warwick nodded his sleek dark head towards the cheering and waving crowds pushing their way into the streets to snatch a glimpse of our company. "Do they sneer and gibe, My Lord? Or do they smile and beam upon us?" As I could not say they were unwelcoming, Warwick continued.

"This is our chance, My Lord, and by nightfall I vow I shall add Highness to your titles!"

Silently I gazed, first at him then at the bustling, jostling crowds. He had always been a determined and convincing man, this cousin of mine, possessed of as much intelligence and insight as his aunt, my mother, herself and, allied to this, he had the strength of a man accustomed to battle and skirmish. Hitherto, he had loyally supported Lancaster, its Queen and King and their 'son'. But our world had changed irrevocably now, the Vixen's vengeance, trickery and arrogance swelling so full that my father had no resort but to battle against her in England's cause. Now Warwick too acknowledged the Prince a Bastard and, it seemed, had set his ambitions' sights upon me. Would his dream include my marriage to his daughter, the delicate Anne? I doubted it, and indeed would say nay to it, for my brother Richard (although but a boy) had spoken to me of his desire to wed Anne. Since they were small they had played together, both so alike in looks and thoughts, dark, slender, studious; it seemed only right they should marry. Dear as my family are to me, I had vowed to do all possible to bring Richard his longed-for bride. Who would be *my* Queen should my cousin's plan succeed? She would need to be comely and passionate; and witty, too, for I had my choice of women and my Queen must be an exceptional creature : one who could hold my attention and my heart. Seriously, I did not believe such a woman existed. (How surprised I was to be!) As we rode, my thoughts glanced over possible brides for a King of England: Catherine of Bourbon, Philip of Burgundy's niece? That would rupture the plans of Charles of France! The ageing Mary of Gueldres, mother of James Second of Scotland? No, she was too ancient for my tastes, and anyway Scotland was not amicable to England. I had to rack my memory for other suitable Princesses, at last recalling that Henry of Castile had a ten year old sister. Isabella. Marriage with a skinny child? I could not countenance that idea, either. Of the three, Catherine seemed the more attractive, but truth to tell I was not content about any.

Glancing at my cousin's aloof face (I never could discern what he was thinking) I imagined his retaliatory remark should I introduce the subject of women. "What? Women first *again*, cousin? I vow the Throne is not yet won but you have a Queen already!" His cool reaction to the ladies often amused, but usually annoyed me, for I failed to understand such disinterest in the delicious, shapely creatures. Surely in all the world there were no more beautiful and appealing wonders than they? I was an eager thirteen when I first bedded a wench—a lively fair girl of the same age who gazed upon me as if I were a god and prattled that she had been deprived of her maidenhead by no less than the Duke of York's heir! 'Twas a goodly encounter for my first, and served to make me hunger for more . . . and more, the which I have had and in great abundance. . . .

Warwick was speaking to me again, telling me that we must announce my claim to the Throne and our grievances against the Monk-King and his Vixen whore whilst we had ripe chance (for Parliament was adjourned, and London was our juicy purple plum to pick). So, he declared, we would ride to those points in London which he had selected as most advantageous to spread our news—Westminster Hall, the Abbey, St Paul's amongst them, at which three points I myself addressed the people, they cheering me loud and long, after which my cousin called to them "Wilt thou have Edward as thy King in place of Henry?" they clamouring, "Yea, yea, King Edward!" My heart seemed to be loose in my chest, throbbing and bouncing, when I heard their determination to have me as their sovereign. So swift, so soon had it all occurred, tragedy giving way to joy, that it was barely believable. If only my father and Edmund had been able to see it, and my mother, too!

Our ears ringing from the cries and cheers, my cousin and I rode to our lodgings and there we feasted generously and, while my cousin slept I explored the curvaceous body of a serving girl, a yellow-haired wench with breasts like melons and nipples like gold coins. That was my method of celebrating!

4th March, 1461, I began my reign, and London still adored me. However, I was not misled by their amity into believing all of England felt likewise. So many factions and disruptions had there been between Lancaster and York that a Yorkist King would not bring smiles to all faces overnight. Sure enough, by March's ending, the Vixen and her mad spouse were facing my army for the appalling battle of Towton, a battle at which thirty-three thousand men bade the world good-bye, weird spring snows drifting down upon their bloody bodies. The Vixen and her weakling husband scampered for Scotland, and I rode in triumph to York—where my father's and brother's heads still hung above the gates—and was there greeted joyously. Now I felt more securely King.

From York we traversed my new Kingdom observing, listening, praising, pardoning and punishing, until we arrived in Northamptonshire—approaching the manor of Lord Rivers, Grafton by name. It was here that I was to meet that exceptional creature who was to become my adored wife and Queen : Elizabeth Wydville, widow of Sir John Grey who was slain at the second battle of St Albans. At Grafton, Lord Rivers awaited me, trembling no doubt as to the degree of punishment which I would serve upon him for he had failed miserably to support my cause during the struggles of the past years, favouring the Vixen and allowing his daughter Elizabeth to be her lady-in-waiting and confidante.

Two days I lingered at Grafton, fully pardoning Lord Rivers much to his astonishment (for a new King needs allies and grateful friends, not bitter enemies). And, whilst hunting in Whittlebury Forest, I first met with the widow Elizabeth, the fragile, yellow-haired beauty who had two sons already yet could have been a maid still. By a great oak, standing in a fanshape of sunlight protruding through its branches she stood, gowned in widow's dense black edged with white coney, her silver-yellow hair flowing loose far down her back, her engraved eyes rich sapphires, her skin porcelain, her lips enamelled rose. A medieval Madonna, a Ceres, a wood nymph, my Elizabeth, my Queen!

Of course I had heard much of him, the new young King Edward of the comely form and handsome face, and I was not downcast by what I saw as he approached me in the Forest. He was handsome; fine-skinned; with almond-shaped blue eyes, a straight and beautiful nose, curvaceous sensual lips, a clear complexion and radiant; and long silken brown hair to his shoulders. He was immensely tall for our day—six feet three I had been told, and straight backed. There was no blemish upon him, nor deformity. Without thinking, I compared him to my dead husband and found there was no comparison.

I cannot say that I had planned (schemed some would call it) to attract the new King with my body. All that I wished was to beg his pity for myself and my family, for I was penniless, newly widowed, and had two young sons in dire need of a protector. Yet, as Edward rode towards me, alert, beautiful and smiling, my widow's grief dropped from me like a cloak and passion I had thought long dead surged within me. Wild-patterned thoughts, all too immodest for a widow, cleaved my mind into fragments and left me bemused and hot-cheeked.

Stepping towards the King who dismounted and walked towards me, I would have spoken, but found my carefully rehearsed pleas for succour dried in my throat. At that second, a fanshape of sunlight burst through the branches of the great oak behind me and flung itself across me. It was like an omen, and my heart settled, then lifted happily. The King was nearly nineteen and marvellous comely. I was twenty-three, and widowed, had proved myself fertile, and was undeniably attractive (it would be vanity to deny that which was the truth and therefore far removed from conceit). Suddenly, like a gate swinging open, I saw the future which might possibly be mine should I desire it. . . .

Jacquetta, my mother, had brought me up to prize the value of my beauty and my brain, she saying I had a more than generous amount of both, and so it was my urge to value myself high now, in the eyes of the gorgeous King of England. He would see a dainty young woman, white-gold hair streaming free, her skin pallid as the petals of a lily, her eyes richly blue as periwinkles, her lips a natural tearose pink . . . and he would think: "She is a widow, and I am unwed . . . and in need of a Queen comely enough to brew love in the hearts of all those who see her. . . ." Thinking thus, I managed to find my voice, a little husky yet melodious as ever, and with it I greeted His Highness, Edward, who was called the Rose of Rouen (at which place he had been born), just as his mother was called the Rose of Raby for her birthplace and her beauty.

The King smiled down upon me as I made low and graceful obeisance, extending the skirts of my black gown upon the forest floor, and then I rose, looking fully upwards at him, directly into his almond-carved dark eyes. The sun had dipped a little and now was extending itself beyond me and upon the head of the new King where it glowed like an aureole of gilt. Recalling what I had heard of the King's new emblem—the Sun in Splendour—I marvelled at the aureole shimmering about his head. Once, he had azure feathers in a crest coronet for his emblem and, for his badge, a white lion, but then had come the battle of Mortimer's Cross. That day, February 2nd, 1461, had occurred a most astonishing spectacle: early in the morning, as the army had prepared for attack, no less than three dazzling suns had appeared in the heavens, stunning all who saw them. At once, the army had identified the three suns with the Holy Trinity, taking them as an omen of victory (which they had later celebrated) and it was said the three suns became one as battle commenced. Lowering my eyes from the aureole, I saw upon the King's breast the emblem of the Sun in Splendour and with it the White Rose of York, the Suns embroidered in gold, the Rose in white silk; fitting badges for a noble King.

As he took my hand in his, bowing over it most gallantly and listening to my request for protection and succour, I forgot that recently I had been lady-in-waiting to Margaret, Queen of the deposed King Henry, and that she had never spoken one good word of the dead Duke of York or his heir whilst in my presence. But she was safe in Scotland, and I was at the new King's mercy; only a fool would have angered the new King, and I most definitely was not a fool! I had two young sons, and was penniless; I had been in favour with the losing side; I was chief confidante of the deposed Queen; the new King had every reason to distrust or repulse me and fling me into the Tower, too, should he so choose. Everything my mother had ever taught me rose in my mind and allied to it was all that I had ever learnt since entering the world of adults and becoming a matron. Jacquetta had told me only the day before that Edward of York was a sensual, passionate man; that he adored women; that he could never resist a comely wench; and I had heard my ex-mistress herself say many times that he was a sybarite and a lecher, her names for him and, as always with Margaret, highly coloured and exaggerated. If only half of what she had said of him were true, he would be possessed of the strength and sexual energies of four men! (Secretly I was hoping he had sufficient for at least two. . . .) And, being thus, he would be easy bait for me, who already knew so much of men and their connivings. Sense and reason informed me that Edward had never been refused by any maid he desired, and that once he had lusted he just as rapidly left. . . . They told me too that I must be different. Not flaunting sexuality—for he had had his fill of sex and easy maids, and had never been deprived of satisfaction. Nor an enamelled and chilly Madonna, for that would be too daunting. Rather should I be myself: lovely, witty, shrewd, perceptive, a complete kaleidoscope of talents and virtues which deeply would enthral and captivate a man who had rarely looked above a woman's breasts. And in his new position as King, he would need advice and heartening, patience and counselling. If I wished to remain high in his thoughts, I must precede all those who thought to woo or win Edward with *amour* or guidance. . . .

We, Edward and I, parted that day with expectation rife within our hearts, he eager to see more of me (so he later told me) and I just as eager to see him again. He had promised me his protection and all the support I should need—both strength and gold—and I did not doubt his words. When, after he had departed, we heard he had endowed my mother with three hundred and thirty-three marks four shillings and a third of a farthing per annum—the amount of her dowry—plus having pardoned my father and forgiven him for all his 'offences and trespasses' against the new King, we knew we could indeed trust Edward of York.

Soon after, we heard of the preparations for Edward's coronation, which was to be 28th June, 1461, and a most splendent affair despite the poverty of the Royal exchequer. Yet, despite all the bustle and activity, I heard no word from the King for many weeks, and gradually I believed he had forgotten me, and I might never see him again, except perhaps about the court should he summon me to wait upon his new Queen when he chose her.

A QUEEN FOR ENGLAND, 1461–64

Now that I had set eyes upon the incomparable Elizabeth Wydville, Catherine of Bourbon, Mary of Gueldres and Isabella of Castile receded into the void. But the demands of my new Crown were exacting, and days fled by without my having contacted Elizabeth. I had pardoned her father, pensioned off her mother, promised her my protection—would that suffice to tell her she would be exceedingly special in my eyes? But perhaps no, for I had pardoned many whilst pursuing my policy of ensuring stout allies for an embryo dynasty. I vowed to contact the lovely widow very soon, relying upon her recent bereavement to keep her safely out of the marriage market until I had time to woo her properly. Meanwhile, I enquired discreetly about her past. Though exceedingly lovely, highly intelligent, and related to the Count of St Pol and the Bishop of Thérouanne, Jacquetta Duchess of Bedford being her mother, she had—like her mother—married low where she might have married high. There had been two scandalous unions in Harry V's time: the remarriage of his widow Catherine de Valois to her groom of the wardrobe, Owen Tudor, and the remarriage of Jacquetta, widow of Harry V's uncle, John Duke of Bedford, to Sir Richard Wydville. Both unions had been illicit and, for their wilful secrecy, Catherine's children were taken from her, and she and her husband put away. Jacquetta had been fined one thousand pounds. Elizabeth was the latter's first child after her remarriage and, in that year of 1437, Catherine de Valois died, as did Queen Joanna, Henry Four's widow, leaving Jacquetta Wydville premier Lady of the land. In 1445, the Duchess and her husband sailed to France to convey the Vixen-Queen and her retinue to England after which Jacquetta became attendant upon the Vixen—her relative by marriage. Some four years later, Sir Richard was endowed with the title of Baron Rivers, soon after to be created a Knight of the Garter and put in command of the Calais garrison for a number of years.

After Elizabeth, twelve more children were born to the

Duchess, and, by all accounts they were a close and devoted family. (This pleased me, for such was our family.) When Elizabeth married her John Grey*—heir to Lord Ferrers of Groby—he was untitled, but won a knighthood at St Albans given him by the Monk-King. I am told theirs was a love match—which fact jostled my tranquillity—and Elizabeth was but sixteen when the ceremony took place. It did not pay her to wed for love, for when she was widowed she lost all—husband, fortune, security. No man who truly and selflessly cherishes and loves his woman would leave her destitute, floundering in poverty, and facing such despair. Silently I called the dead knight knave and other harsher names, vowing I would treat the Lady better when I won her. (At that point, brash with youth and passion, I did not doubt I would gain her love.)

At the deposing of the Monk-King, Lord Rivers and his sons were on the losing side, Jacquetta feared the loss of her dowry and saw no hope of gaining her other daughters good matches, and the fair Elizabeth was widowed and penniless. However, they were already aware of my bounty and no longer trembling with dread of my vengeance. This way are powerful allies created! When Elizabeth became my Queen, I would have the entirety of her large family my ardent followers, and all their relatives and friends likewise. A wise move—yet thought of it had arrived only after I had set eyes on the marvellous fair Lady of Whittlebury Forest, the gilt-haired hamadryad who would soon warm my bed and curve her body to mine. At mere thought of it, my body heated, my lust swelled.

* He was Lady Jane Grey's great great grandfather.

Edward, my beloved, swiftly compensated for his silence following our first meeting. Soon after his crowning, passionate and promising letters began to arrive, and then my parents were invited to court, I with them. In all those letters, though heated and explicit, Edward never spoke of legal union, for (as I later discovered) his conniving cousin, Warwick, was busy planning a grand French marriage for him and, while his cousin—now called Kingmaker—strove to make terms with France, Edward delighted in secretly strewing his own scheme. Yet, if he had thought to make easy marriage with me, his mother had other mind!

Proud Cis thought me beneath her son, and duly told him so in no meagre terms, the which conversation he later related to me.

"My son," she said (so Edward told me) her cheeks flaming, "I cannot see how you came to this idea of marrying one of your own subjects, and that a poor widow! You are newly enthroned, and an alliance with a rich foreign Princess would be admirable for England. One day, you may well inherit her fortune and lands, endowing England with further possessions."

To which Edward replied: "She is a widow, and already has children, and by God's Blessed Lady I am a bachelor, yet have some too, so we each possess proof that neither shall be barren. And therefore, Madame, I pray thou be content. I trust in God she shall bring a young Prince to play on your lap to your great pleasure, and then you will be most content and bless my Queen."

With rising spirit (for she was furious to be ignored) Proud Cis said, "If you refuse to heed me, bring in the Lady Elizabeth Lucy and make her your Queen, for you have had many a wanton dalliance with her, and you enticed her to your bed by telling her there was a contract of marriage betwixt you both!"

Edward did as he was bid, for he had nothing to fear from this quarter and duly Elizabeth Lucy entered their presence and was questioned by Proud Cis upon her union with her son.

Blushing, Lady Lucy had to admit that she had allowed Edward to bed with her on promise of a contract between them, and not on proof of one existing. "His Grace spoke so lovingly, My Lady, that I dearly hoped he would soon wed me, and that was the only reason I allowed him access to my bed. Had he not, I would never have agreed."

I laughed upon hearing Edward relate the scene so honestly, and it further strengthened me in my endeavour to remain out of his bed until the marriage which would make me his Queen. No idle dalliance for me, after which to be cast aside as Lady Lucy and so many others had been! A man like Edward does not value a woman who is easily laid. As yet, he had no notion that I would prove difficult to woo, for as yet he had not spoken directly to me of marriage! It seemed everyone in his Kingdom knew he wished to wed me except Warwick and myself!

The children Edward had spoken of, namely his two bastards to Lady Lucy, were Elizabeth and Arthur Plantagenet—his only two bastards so far. Well aware was I that I might bear him two more at least, and then be put aside like Lady Lucy to linger and languish until death snatched me, a poor widow still, and without a crown. A callous fate, and one which I refused to allow. My children by Edward would be Royal, or I would not bear them!

Meanwhile, Warwick strove to win the French Princess for Edward, hoping thereby to woo crafty Louis XI's aid where now he lavished it upon Queen Margaret and Prince Edward (I still name them thus, for I served Margaret loyally until Edward's love captured me; I find it hard to call her Vixen and her son Bastard as Edward so eagerly does). At the time, Louis the Spider gave Margaret a small fleet and meagre army to help her win back her Throne, but they were French ships and French soldiers and she a French woman—hated by the English. At first she succeeded in taking three castles, Bamborough, Dunstanborough, and Alnwick, then was she met by the full force of Edward's and Warwick's armies, who rapidly put down her men, causing her to flee destitute—yet still arrogant—to her father's court in Lorraine where we heard naught of her for seven years after.

This threat reversed, Edward returned victorious, yet it was 1464 before finally we were able to wed, Warwick later being appeased at the rebuttal of his French plan, and Proud Cis a little more amiable (though unwilling to show it!). Bona of Savoy would never be Queen of England now! And I had kept my vow to stay chaste until I became Queen, though Edward—naturally—tried his utmost to persuade me into lechery! And with every refusal from me, his passion flamed the stronger, his eagerness to wed me growing and swelling until he asked me formally to marry him. I accepted, and yet resisted his ardour all the more! Which greatly puzzled him. . . .

There were other matters to plan, too, for I had two sons by my slain husband, and their future must be secured. One, Thomas, was to marry the unborn daughter of the King's chamberlain, Lord Hastings, and the second, Richard, was to marry the unborn daughter should Thomas die in the meantime. (Failing Lord Hastings siring this daughter, one of his brother's unborn daughters, or the daughters of Anne Ferrers, his sister.) Such manors as might become the property of Richard and Thomas, half of the rent and profits thereof while Thomas or (if he died) Richard was under the age of twelve years, were to belong to Lord Hastings and half to myself. Lord Hastings would pay me 500 marks on the marriage, but should both my sons die before then, or should there be no daughter born, I was to pay Hastings 250 marks. He, a man of strength and loyalty, was most capable of protecting my two boys, for he was the King's confidant, and most influential a Lord.

It was now approaching the First day of May, 1464, this being the day Edward and I were to marry in secret at Grafton.

* * *

'In moste secret manner upon the fyrste day of May kynge Edward spoused Elizabeth late the wyfe of syr Johan Graye knyghte . . . and which spousayles were solempnised erely in the morninge at a towne named Grafton nere unto Stonynge-stratforde. At whyche maryage was no persones

present, but the spousesse, the Duches of Bedford her mother, the preste two gentyl women, & a young man to helpe the preste synge.'

* * *

The ceremony was smooth and swift, naught causing delay or query; my mother's filbert eyes were bright upon me as she watched my husband the King of England looping my marriage finger with the circle of heavy gold which would pronounce me his. Yet, though we were wed, there was to be no whisper of our union until Edward deemed the moment right, for Warwick was still negotiating for Bona of Savoy, and I fear would have been vexed to hear his sovereign had espoused a subject for then Warwick would never be called Queen-Maker. . . .

I wore a sumptuous gown of azure velvet, scoop necked, high waisted, with trailing hem befurred with Royal ermine and a hennin of studded gold tissue with veil of azure gauze. The gems about my narrow neck were sapphires bedded in gold and, beneath, a chain of goldsmith's exquisite work, on which dangled a great glossy pearl the shape of a pear : all gifts from my King. I wore soft-blue colouring upon my lids, and rouge-rose upon my lips, with kohl from the East to darken my lashes, for Edward prefers paint upon his women. The cuffs and breast-collar of my gown were gold tissue embroidered with pearls, sapphires, gold thread and minute gold beads; the heavy wedding aureole hung upon my tiny finger, weighting my hand, constantly reminding me I was now Queen of England. . . .

When we were silent and alone in our conjugal chamber that night, Edward disrobed with scarlet cheeks and shaking fingers, to reveal to me his magnificent and powerful body, the muscles fully developed yet by no means bulky and overlarge (which I would have abhorred), his shoulders wide and manly above his narrow, sculpted waist and flat stomach, the gold hairs curling thickly low upon that stomach, the crown for his sumptuous masculinity. . . .

I was left in no doubt as to my husband's prowess and stamina, for he took me no less than six times that night, scything my body joyfully and energetically. Momentarily, a sculling memory of my first husband's indolent lovemaking pranced through my mind and vanished never to return. No woman could ever ponder upon another man's sexuality after lying with Edward Plantagenet. . . .

He called me his Rose Queen and his May Queen, told me I would be pregnant of our son before the night was through and lavished tenderness and lust upon me in extraordinary quantity. There are men one can learn to love; others who can never be loved however hard one tries; men who strive to earn one's love, and men—so rare—like Edward who are cherished and adored from first sight and can be forgiven all faults—men one can never leave or exist without. After Whittlebury Forest, I had known my life would shrink to naught should Edward leave me. . . .

So we were wedded and bedded, and only a quartet knew of it. Later, when Warwick was pacified, and England more pacific, Edward would have me crowned and fêted in the London streets. I could not wait!

From my bed, Edward travelled to York spending the next two moons in Yorkshire, then on to London (pausing to visit me) to the Chilterns, to Stamford, back to the Chilterns and his manor of Penley, from whence he visited Woodstock frequently. When London saw him again that autumn he was cornered by his Council on the subject of his choosing a Queen; to which he replied with his adorable smile that he had done this already: choosing one who was both exceptionally beautiful, witty and fertile: Elizabeth Wydville, daughter of Lord Rivers and the Duchess of Bedford. There must have been grimaces and frowns then, I vow! Their new and beloved King had selected a daughter of the Vixen's confidants and allies as his spouse! What consternation this must have caused! Yet they knew my husband's way: he believed in forgiving and forgetting, not bearing grudges nor harbouring revenge. (Thanks be to the Blessed Virgin!) So it was made public, and though hatred was culled in many, I was pronounced Queen in Reading Abbey on Michaelmas Day, 1464, being led into the Abbey by the glowering Warwick, and the Duke of Clarence, my brother in law. (He whose vacuous smile seemed to pronounce favourably towards me; but as yet I did not know this same vacuous smile was ever upon his lips; he was, too, a drunkard and a sot, and his arm shook where I clasped it with my hand, the trembling being caused by some emotion other than lust or fear. . . .)

Observing the faces in the Abbey, hovering whitely above glittering robes and gems, I saw many expressions and few pleasant. There were scowls and frowns, twisted mouths and dipping brows, tight lips and hostile eyes, a few smiles which bordered upon nervous smirks, and one or two genuinely pleased at Edward's obvious joy, his mother not among them. . . . After, there were public announcements regarding our marriage earlier that year, and great celebrating amongst the people for, whether or not they loved me the wine conduits flowed and there were meat and bread and ale despatched in the streets, there being naught like free food to mellow an Englishman.

In truth, though Warwick sulked, he knew it was better for me to be the new King's match than a French Princess, for England had sickened of Frenchness and French marriages, the Vixen still lurking horribly in its thoughts. And soon my own knowledge of so much hostility towards me paled as plans for my coronation leapt into life. Amongst these was an invitation to my uncle, Jacques de Luxembourg, Seigneur de Richeburg, to our court, he being requested to bring with him some hundred guests—of any birth but French. My uncle Jacques, the youngest of my mother's three brothers, had been Arthur of Brittany's second-in-command when the great Arthur was Constable of France and Duke of Brittany. From all accounts, he was a vigorous and splendid man.

Even before my crowning, I intended to make it clear I wished to be served as grandly and obediently as all Queens before me. Reluctance, hostility or disobedience I would not allow in my presence, knowing fully I could rely upon my husband to support me in every one of my desires. He, meanwhile, was preparing for the coronation with great diligence and eagerness. From one John Hedlain, he had purchased two bay coursers and a white courser for my carriage, these costing 50 marks. Elyn Langworth, a silk embroiderer, received £27.5 shillings for materials she created for my chariot, saddle and pillion, and John Cornish received £168.18 shillings for articles to be used by me (he being a sadler). Of course, Westminster Abbey was to be the venue for my crowning and, at my instigation, Edward was to insist that the ceremony be more excellent and vivid than any which had gone before. Meanwhile I was carefully selecting and planning my wardrobe for the occasion.

After it was known I was Edward's Queen, forward pranced the suitors for my sisters' hands, Margaret being wooed by Lord Maltravers, heir of the Earl of Arundel, Anne by William Bourchier, the Earl of Essex's heir, Jacquetta by John Lord Strange, Joan by Anthony Grey of Ruthin, heir of the Earl of Kent, Catherine by the parents of young Henry, Duke of Buckingham—they both to be carried in arms at the ceremony—baby Mary by the parents of William Herbert (later to become Earl of Pembroke), baby Martha by Sir John Bromley, and my brother, John, was wed to the ancient Catherine, Duchess of Norfolk, my husband's aunt, he being her fourth husband. Anthony had married four years before, to Lady Scales, he duly taking this title by right. Richard showed not one jot of passion for women—or for men!

On April 14th, Edward despatched a letter to the Mayor of London, saying, '*We have certainly appointed and concluded the Coronation of our most dear and most entirely beloved wife the Queen to be at our Palace at Westminster upon the Sunday before Whitsun next coming: we will and pray you that at the said day and place ye for that cause give your personal attendance there in such apparel as is according to your estate and honour. And that ye leave not this in any wise.*' It was good to know I was so warmly loved and that my new husband was determined my crowning would be glorious.

They were days of loving and laughter, richness and joy. Edward was as attentive as only he could be, kissing my hands and my fingertips, my forehead and my neck, never greeting me without his arms bulging with gifts, his mouth asmile. I had gems as bulky and vivid as an Empress's, robes sumptuous and studded with jewels, their hems dragging along the rush-strewn floors, made heavy by the lengths of ermine and sable attached. My hands were encrusted with rings, my fingers so stiff with them that I could scarce bend them at the knuckles, and had I worn every one of the neck chains Edward gave me I would have been unable to raise my head! Atop these gifts were merchants brought to show me their most splendid wares: purple silks and velvets, damasks, tissues of gold and silver, cloth of gold blinding in its brilliance, gauzes for my hennins so fine and translucent that they were barely visible, furs from the East, glossy, thick and dense, coronals of buttercup gold embedded with gems of every hue and shape, mantles of velvet embossed with gold embroidery so intricate it seemed to have been woven as one with the material, slippers narrow and dainty, sewn in softest, smoothest kids, and sewn again with pearls and rubies, gold buckles and laces. The Vixen-Queen (as I now called her, Edward's nickname being now familiar to me) had never owned such riches as these! We were astride a new age, riding to marvels and miracles, and I as Queen of the Sun King of York in my fantastic crowning array would be first of these marvels and miracles to astonish and astound the citizens of London.

I did not tarry with nervousness, fretting about the day itself; rather did I eagerly await it. There was no doubt in me that I would acquit myself most ably, and further strengthen the Yorkist Crown in England. No man would ever find need to say that a King's subject—taken to wife as his Queen—could not bear herself every jot as brilliantly and gracefully as a Royal Princess from one of the great Houses of Christendom.

That Friday arrived which was to see me formally become Queen of Edward Fourth, and I left Eltham Palace to journey by road to the city which awaited me in grand festive mood. By Shooters Hill I was greeted by the Mayor and Aldermen splendently garbed in crimsons and golds, their faces alight with genuine pleasure. These latter conducted me proudly through Southwark (where King Cade-Mortimer had so recently reigned) and onwards to the Tower where I was, like other sovereigns soon to be crowned, to spend the night, on my way to the Tower there being various amusements to entertain me and prove the citizens' loyalty and love. At London Bridge a clerk robed as St Paul approached me bearing words of welcome, and from one of the houses sitting squatly on the Bridge floated disembodied voices, sweetly singing. Further on my journey my litter halted before a great stage which, the Mayor proudly told me, had taken many weeks and much toil to complete. Eight men had laboured for twelve days on the stage itself, and five thousand nails had been used in the construction, after which two men had worked for fifteen days to cover the scaffolding with ninety-six ells of material; then the stage had been painted and stained, and decorated with streamers and variehued papers of white and gold, black, green and red. With immense delight, the Mayor informed me of every detail appertaining to the stage, obviously intending that I should be fully aware of the vast trouble and expense to which the city was prepared to go for the Queen of the Sun King of York. The stage had been erected to bear eight effigies, six being women and two angels, all garbed in purple and scarlet buckram, flax wigs dyed with saffron upon their heads, the angels' wings being made with nine hundred peacocks' feathers. Also, there were two men guised as saints—one, in my honour, St Elizabeth, the other St Mary Cleophas, whose Day it was. St Elizabeth uttered a speech of welcome to me, after which, impressed by the stage and all upon it, I was borne in my litter to the Chapel of St Thomas à Becket, guardian of the City of London, inside which sang a choir, as inside St Magnus' Church beyond.

The voices of the choirs, the hubbub of the crowd, was like a golden dinning in my ears, and nowhere that I gazed did I see a gloomy or sour expression. How difficult to believe that only months before the Vixen had reigned here with her mad husband, and London had bowed to her every whim! Within, though glad that I now had London's goodwill, I was aware that a city which can honour can just as swiftly dishonour . . . they had once knelt to the Mad King, yet now they knelt to the Sun King. . . . Would they, if Fate journeyed onwards as before and, as so often is said, repeated itself, one day reject the Sun King and myself in favour of others? A dart of chilliness pierced my heart, then just as quickly vanished. I was foolish to be pessimistic on my Crowning Day! This day was to be the heralder of thousands more when I and my Edward reigned and ruled supreme—he, tall magnificent and fearless would not allow his Throne to be snatched away from him as whining, wailing Henry had!

Now excitement pulsed beneath my skin, for my adored

husband had awaited me for two days in the Tower itself, and my eyes craved to see him again, my body aching for union with his. Never, if I had not lain with Edward, would I have guessed at the depths of lust coursing within me . . . he had awakened passion and desire sufficient for two women and now, when others might have dwelt on naught but the ceremonies to come, all I could think upon was Edward taking me in his arms, pressing his strong yet velvet-soft body against mine.

Edward the Sun King greeted me in brilliant garb, gold and scarlet velvet vying with satin of the same hues. How tall he appeared as I stepped from my litter into his arms, and received his kisses upon my cheeks! Surely there were few in London as tall or as magnificent as my husband the King? As I gazed up at his flushed face, I was as giddy as a young maid, knowing full well that his thoughts too dwelt upon that eve when we would bed together in the Tower.

This was a secret pleasure—atop the one of anticipation—which only we shared, we each knowing the other thought of bedding and not solely of the crowning, whilst all around us stood crowds of cheering and jogging Londoners believing we pondered in stately fashion upon the ceremony and naught else!

Like eager young lovers we passed through the noisy, excited crowds and into the Tower itself where the Royal apartments had been splendently decorated for this very occasion. So sumptuous were they that I found myself dazzled by the gold and crimson, purple and gilt, yet, despite the magnificence, the apartments were chill—a fact caused by the Palace's proximity to the River. There was none of the airy pleasantry of Eltham or Sheen in this dank Tower—which was also used to house traitors—and had I not been full occupied with Edward's attention that eve I would, I vow, have been sore depressed. Some gloom about the place struck at my heart—it was as if I had known great misery here—yet I had not, having as yet little time to grow accustomed to its venue. However, dismissing such thoughts was easy when my husband ordered fine wines and delicacies to be brought us, he then banishing the servants and taking me upon his knee. We were by the great hearth where a vast fire blazed, and close by was the sideboard laden with meats and wines, cakes and pastries. Every comfort had been provided, and had I strained my mind I could not have found myself short of any indulgence. It was good being Queen!

Edward was not hindered in his objectives by the heavy ornate robes which clasped my body. Tearing aside the brooches and fastenings, he flung my mantle to the rushes, soon my gown following it. Gazing at me in my kirtle of transparent lawn, he clacked his tongue as if teasingly then pressed hard, determined kisses upon my cheeks and neck and breasts, catching the fine lawn in his strong fingers and ripping it from my breasts.

"These fashions which demand such luscious breasts be pressed flat inside a lady's gown!" he complained. "Why hide such bountiful fruits, Madame?"

"Would you have me walk free about the court with my breasts loose for all to see?" I teased. "Imagine Warwick's sour face if he saw such bawdiness before him!" (I spoke lightly of Warwick, hiding my hatred of him. He had made Edward King, yet he was arrogant enough to think himself King, and I a jumped-up commoner.)

"I vow Warwick looks sour because he has *not* seen such beauty!" murmured my husband, scooping each of my breasts in his palms and taking my nipples between his forefinger and thumb—which action drove me swift into ecstasy. Seconds later, I was urging him to carry me to the great bed, and there he flung himself atop of me with all the passion and strength of a young yet highly experienced lover. More seconds, and I was reaching that stage of crescendo which Edward had shown me since our marriage and which, before, I had never guessed at. And then, not allowing me to rest, Edward was returning me to the cherished state of ecstasy, ever considerate of my needs above his.

Though my own marital experience had been limited before I met Edward, there had been many snippets to reach my ears of selfish husbands, arrogant and cruel—even bestial—who would ever place their own lusts first, centre, and last. There were many, gossip informed me, who drank to danger point then made vile onslaughts upon their terrified wives; others who did not need to drink to adopt the habits and behaviour of the lowest animal; still more who were—whilst not vicious—inconsiderate and careless of their spouses' satisfaction. How many women could say their husbands had made them far more of a woman than they could ever have thought possible? How many could have expected such delight as Edward gave me every time we came together?

It lies in a man's hands to create his own woman : he can make her nervous, fretful, fearful; or he can make her cynical, disloyal, reluctant. Or, too, he can render her faithful grateful, joyous, ever supporting him; ever devoted. Even these few short weeks with Edward had shown me the future course of my reaction to him : despite the anxieties of battle and Kingship he had toiled lovingly over me, intent upon my desire, knowing the first weeks of new love and new marriage can never be repeated and may affect a lifetime together. And thus he had ensured (without realising it) that my heart and my mind would ever be his, in every sphere, in every possibility. I know that our enemies have fretted and puzzled at my devotion to Edward—and his to me—wondering why I have continued to love and adore him despite his infidelities, his many mistresses; and, should they dare to ask me why then I would not tell them. Suffice it to say that never once have I been left dissatisfied or unsatisfied because of Edward's *affaire* with any other woman. As though I were a sundial clearly showing to him alone my intimate needs, he has gauged them and satisfied me lovingly. I have never (like so many of our enemies' wives) lain cold and frustrated in my bed awaiting my husband's return from whoring. If by naught else then the frequency of my conceiving has proved Edward's attentiveness. (And that too has perturbed our enemies!)

Next day, at dawn's peak, Edward flung wide the casement, inhaling the May air with vigour (the River is lovely in May—by July it stinks) then he called me to his side, and we embraced as eagerly as though we had just met and the previous eve had never been. When the servants came to garb us for the day, they found us abed once more, deep beneath the coverlets! And then it was time for us to don the composure and solemnity expected of us along with the trailing robes of sovereignty. After a last kiss I entered my horse-borne litter and began the journey to Westminster with an escort composed of those new Knights of the Bath whom Edward had recently created in my honour—they wearing blue gowns and hoods of white silk. Again, the Londoners were out in droves to cheer me, many of their remarks loudly voiced, floating up to me in my decorously-moving litter.

"That gold silk hair!"

"She'll have lovely boys for York!"

"How tiny she is—like a doll! a Royal doll!"

"The fairest Queen we've ever had in our city!"

"They say the King met her in a forest in a fairy dell, and he calls her his Fairy Queen! Now I see why—she's all white and gold like Mab herself!" (Later, when the fickle Londoners had decided I was not to their liking, the stories of the fairy dell were deformed into ones where I was a sorceress guised as a fairy intent upon bewitching and enslaving their innocent young King. Edward finds the gossip highly amusing, "If you were wall-eyed or hump-backed you might have needed magic to catch me, my precious, but radiant beauty never needed more than that to get itself a man!" However, I cannot share his amusement—though I try. Too loud in my ears ring the abusive slanders regarding the Vixen when she reigned, and I care not to be similarly abused.)

But for now the city adored me with full energy and vigour, the sun shone, birds caroled, and blossom beaded the trees with ivory and rose, and I was to be crowned Queen of England!

George, trembling Duke of Clarence, himself and his horse garbed in gold-spangled robes, was first to ride into Westminster Hall he being Steward for the occasion. After him came the Constable and Butler, Arundel, and the Marshal, Norfolk, both of whose mounts were draped in cloth of gold. It was these three who separated the gawping, dazed-eyed crowds so that I might walk into the Hall beneath a canopy of cloth of gold hung with silver-gilt bells, the Bishop of Salisbury on my left, the Bishop of Durham on my right, my robe a splendent purple, a gold coronet upon my loosened hair. Behind, came the Abbot of Westminster, and my train was borne by Edward's aunt, the Duchess of Buckingham, who was followed into the Hall by two of Edward's sisters, the Duchess of Suffolk and the Lady Margaret; his mother, proud and haughty of mien as always; the Duchess of Bedford, and the rest of the Ladies. (How it must have irked Proud Cis to walk demurely behind me, all eyes fixed on my face and gown and few upon hers!)

The sceptre of St Edward I carried in my right hand, and in my left the sceptre of the Realm, as I walked down the Hall on a cloth of ray, my feet bare, towards that cloister whose door would lead me into the North Transept, and there Clarence and the other Lords dismounted and re-formed before me, accompanied by the brightly-clad *mêlée* which formed the procession. Thirteen Duchesses—my youngest sister amongst them—were in the company in vivid gowns of scarlet velvet and ermine, after them coming fourteen Baronesses in scarlet and miniver, and all the while the silver-gilt bells jangled sweetly on my canopy and the crowds stared, awed and silent, impressed with the solemnity of the occasion.

From the North door, we walked through the Choir to the High Altar and there I knelt whilst the Archbishop of Canterbury read suitable words over me, after which I prostrated myself upon the floor as prayers were said, much as if I were about to become a nun. Now young maidens clustered round me to remove my coronet (their faces pale and solemn) and then the Archbishop anointed me preparatory to my being enthroned upon the waiting chair, where the Abbot of Westminster and the Earl of Essex waited upon me, handing me my sceptres which I clasped whilst the Gospel was intoned. When I went to the High Altar to make my offering, the Abbot and the Earl relieved me of the sceptres, each carrying one before me, and the Duchess of Bedford and the Duchess of Suffolk assisted me by securing the heavy crown upon my head when the responses of the ceremony required me to avert my neck. The *Te Deum* sung, the ceremony within the Abbey was complete, and we re-formed to proceed back the way we had come, through the Hall and into the Palace itself.

My head was aching with the weight of the crown, my shoulders with the dragging robes, and I welcomed being able to retire at this moment into a chamber prepared for me. There I was divested of the cumbersome ceremonial robes, and regarbed in an overgown of rich dense purple be-furred with dazzling ermine, before returning to the Hall to be seated in honour at the crowning banquet, Edward's sisters and the Archbishop of Canterbury beside me. George (his hands shaking as ever) held out the bowl for me to wash—a magnificent bowl of heavy gold—and then I began to eat, finding myself ravenous after the long and strenuous ceremonies. The gesture I had made for the feasting to begin heralded the beginning of the hubbub which rapidly rose for the Hall was crammed with merrymakers: the Mayor and his aldermen, city officers and citizens at one table, Royal relatives at another, churchmen at another, and at the fourth Judges, Barons and various men of law.

Edward had done me proud, for seventeen dishes comprised the first course alone, and every course was ushered in with great ceremonial and pomp. The second course possessed nineteen dishes, the third fifteen, and there was not a morsel ill-cooked, shoddily arranged, or unpleasant to the tongue. Wafers and Hippocras refreshed us after the third course, and then my Chaplain and Almoner removed the cloth from my table so that I might wash, which I did, slowly and decorously. Now it was time for the spice plates to be brought out, they being borne—like other dishes—by the newly-created Knights of the Bath, some of whom were prospective husbands for my marriageable sisters. I ate of the comfits upon the plates—though I vow I had small room for them after the feast—and then the Mayor approached me bearing a gold cup in which was the Wine of Void. I drank, thanked the Mayor and his aldermen for their splendid efforts on my behalf then departed the Hall—walking beneath the cloth of gold canopy with the four tinkling silver-gilt bells, which was supported as before by the Barons of the Cinque Ports. On reaching the door of my chamber I thanked all those who accompanied me, and they departed, bowing with flushed faces.

Twilight was scooping the city into its arms as the Mayor and his fellow officers and the other crowning-guests made for their barges upon the River and were rowed home, replete and content of mind. *Largesse* was distributed amongst the large company of musicians who had entertained me at the banquet, and then all fell quiet, that eerie silence ensuing which falls after great activity and bustle. I was weary, my head ached, my neck too, for I had been expected to keep my back straight throughout the ceremony and the banquet, the massive crown upon my head so that all present might feast their eyes whilst they feasted their stomachs. But now I could rest, lying upon a couch, pressing from my mind thoughts of the later revelry to come: the great tournament here on Monday, when Knights from Burgundy and Luxembourg would vie for the prize of a ruby ring, the many public appearances I must make, always smiling, always cool yet affable (a difficult state to acquire when not born to it. And although Edward says I am more Royal than he in bearing my enemies call it arrogance now!).

Ormond's Inn at Smithfield had been made ready for me after the ceremony and, when rested, I journeyed there to reside, and to establish my household. The Archbishop of Canterbury (always loyal to Edward) had a brother, Lord Berners, and he was my new Chamberlain. My Master of Horse was John Wydville, my two Carvers were James Haute and Sir Humphrey Bourchier, and my two chief attendants were my sister Anne (recently married to Sir Humphrey), and our sister-in-law Elizabeth, wife to our brother, Anthony, Lord Scales. Other attendants were Lady Elizabeth Ovedale, Lady Joanna Norris, and Lady Alice Fogge, and nine lesser women for menial tasks. My Confessor was Edward Story, Cambridge University's Chancellor (and later to become Bishop of Carlisle), and I had my own physician, my Chancellor, lawyer, attorney-general, minstrels, and clerk of the signet. I even had my own council chamber near the Exchequer, in the New Tower!

And I had Edward's love, that meaning more to me than pomp and display, gems and furs. In those days, I would have given up every treasure—every power I had as Queen—to keep his devotion close unto me.

So my fair Elizabeth was duly crowned, and London took her to its generous heart, though there was one blotch I cared not to think upon: capricious and wilful Warwick, offended that I renounced his French marriage plans to Bona of Savoy, and distressed that I had declared I would be no puppet King but would reign alone, unaided, had refused to attend my darling's coronation. He did not like her—that was plain—and I could see no place in my friendship or my Kingdom for a man who failed to bestow due respect and courtesy towards my beloved Queen. He was a fool, Warwick! They called him Kingmaker because he had supported me and planned my accession, assisting in every respect towards that end once he had decided I would be King, yet now he sulked and flamed because I would not humble myself before his will, marry his French Princess and say yea and nay where he would have me say them. Did he think me another Henry Six? I am as unlike him in every way as an eagle from a starling! And mean to prove it! Warwick could go hang himself for his insolence!

Yet there was no public rivalry between us at this time—it was too soon as yet to show such division to England. Apparently, in the people's eyes, Warwick had good excuse to be absent from the crowning, for he was negotiating with Spider Louis in France, only he and I knowing that he had ignored his invitation to the ceremony. This Louis, son of Charles of France, was manacled by fate, and could not broadcast his true feelings at my rejection of the French Princess for he was in desperate need of England's aid. His vassal, the Duke of Burgundy, had allied himself with the Duke of Brittany and other Lords against Louis, forming the League of the Public Weal, their intention being to grasp more power and riches, and appropriate the possessions of France's King.* Louis had nowhere to turn but England and

* In 1464 the King of France did not rule the united France we know today. In 1477 Louis seized the Franche Comté, and Burgundy reverted to the French Crown in the absence of heirs male, likewise the Somme towns. Louis' army seized Arras and Artois, and Anjou and Maine came to him peaceably, with Provence, as did Cerdagne and Roussillon.

Warwick was agreeing to support him in my name on the understanding that he, Louis, refused all further help to the Vixen-Queen in her cause.

When negotiations had been satisfactorily concluded, Warwick returned to England and then the troubles really began! He would have his way, and I would have mine, and these were often diverse though I struggled to keep clarity of mind and not behave contrarily for the sake of it, petulance being more acceptable in young pretty women, not in new Kings. But Warwick would have it that I was petulant—and demanding—and sulky—and untempered as rough steel (which latter may well have been true in those early days). He had no tact about him, demanding where he should have gently led, thinking to be my tutor instead of my companion. Naturally, being young and fiery of temperament, I bridled harshly beneath his impositions, and shortly we were unable to exchange even a minimum of words without fury punctuating them. This then was the finale of that great relationship—King and Kingmaker—which had thrilled England's imagination for many a month, it now being naught but argument, dissent, fury, and—eventually—hatred.

It had to end, for I had seen the repulsive sight of a King roughly dominated by men and by his Queen; he being fearful, trembling, and totally controlled by those exterior to him. That, I had long ago vowed, would never be *me*. All those years in England as a child, my father absent, I hearing all the tales of Henry and his Amazon spouse, had inculcated in me the desire to be ever independent, ever free of advisers who sought more than a mere advisory capacity in my court. No one would rule me, thereby thinking to rule England through me. *No one!* (Later, when my fair Elizabeth revealed her skill for governing and advising, I admit I allowed her free rein for she was my loyal, lovely spouse, yet even when altering my mind upon some matter by her cajolery, she would not have sought to rise above me, her husband; this I knew, and therefore had no fear of her efforts. Indeed, gazing back along the years, I think my reign would have been a cold and isolated thing had she not been my wife and Queen.

Had scheming Warwick and his envious minions thought

to sneer about my Queen not bringing forth an heir for two years following our marriage, their malice was dealt a blow in February, 1466, when our lovesome daughter Elizabeth was born at Westminster, being christened in its Abbey. Prior to her birth, we had been assured the child would be a boy, and one especially, Master Dominic, insisted the child would be a Prince. (Later, we conjured great amusement, for Master Dominic, determined to be the first to inform the King he had a son, had waited without the birthing chamber for the babe's premier cry. On hearing it, he had called, "Pray tell me what the Queen hath, boy or girl?" His reply from one of the Ladies had been, "Whatsoever the Queen's grace hath here within, sure it is that a fool standeth there without!" Speared by the dilemma this answer caused him, Master Dominic had scurried into hiding!)

There was not one astrologer who did not say the Princess would one day wear the Crown, this bringing Elizabeth and myself intense joy. (Yet fear, too, for there had never been a Queen Regnant of England save the Empress Matilda with her brief and discordant reign, her Crown to be taken by Stephen eventually. Would Elizabeth be strong and doughty enough to rule in this vicarious, vicious age?)

With the Princess's birth, we were the more firmly entrenched upon the Throne, and shortly received an abundance of visits from foreign ambassadors whose masters were eager for alliance, friendship or business with us. Too, came planetary visitations, comets in 1468 and 1469, yet none as startling as the one which had appeared in Henry Six's reign, during the month of June. Yet, two comets were preferable to one, however brilliant, and added much power to my hand. The first comet, in 1468, appeared as a blazing star in the west, some four feet high, passing from west to south towards the evening, and showing for some five to six weeks. The second was a blazing star in the west, with a fiery brilliance shaped like a spearhead. Common man accepted the visitations from Heaven as pleasure and support for Edward Four and his beauteous Queen, and their embryo dynasty. With Heaven speaking so dazzlingly what man would dare fault me, or question my right to reign? Only one as arrogant and foolhardy as the Earl of Warwick!

I pleased my Queen immensely by creating her father Earl

and Treasurer after the Princess's birth, he now being Lord Rivers (and, time would prove, an excellent choice for this post). However, whilst I was well served at home, multiple omens declaring a fortuitous reign, and my beloved Queen quickened again, it came to my ears that Warwick was furthering his own cause with crafty Louis, England's cause being neglected. From France came news of Warwick's being splendently fêted by Louis and his court, to a degree far above his position as my adviser, he culling such attentions that it would seem he were King of England and not I. By what I heard of Louis' reaction to him, and by what I read in reports coming to me out of France, it seemed Louis did indeed look upon dark-visaged Warwick as King, and afforded him every favour relevant to this position. An older and more amiable sovereign than I would have balked at this state of affairs! I was not the only one to imagine Warwick was busily furthering his own schemes in France when he should have been furthering mine, and my Queen—ever astute—hinted to me that the Kingmaker may well have intentions of supporting the Vixen and her beaten brood, perhaps plotting with Louis and the Vixen to dethrone me and place either himself or the Bastard Edward as crowned King. (I could see him entrenching the Vixen's son upon the Throne, and calling himself Regent when in fact he was able, by dint of the boy's minority, to wield all power in England. History is peopled with men who grapple to ambition's height then seek to top the Mountain of Sensibility and fall crashing down into the Abyss of Ill Fortune. The Vixen had two such men as her lovers. If Warwick did not perceive the truth regarding his position, and the font from which his strength came, then there could be no ending for him but one similar to those suffered by the Vixen's lovers. That star which can ascend so swiftly can also descend.)

Warwick's star began its downward drop when news was brought me of something Louis had said in France : "They tell me that they have two rulers in England—Monsieur de Warwick and another whose name I have forgotten." Had my pride not been pierced by this remark, I would yet have raged at it. Did Louis—and the rest of Christendom—believe I was another weakly Henry Six trailing, trembling and bemused, behind Warwick's upright, commanding figure? It would seem so, and as such a twisted picture of the King of England was likely to encourage those tragedies which had tortured the country in Henry Six's reign, I could waste no time in showing myself as not only strong but self-sufficient, wise and fearless!

From his visit to France, Warwick returned to my court with French ambassadors, but I refused to see or acknowledge their presence, and when Warwick attempted to speak with me regarding the alliance with France against those countries which had formed the League of the Common Weal (Berry, Bourbon, Brittany, and Burgundy) I was adamant in supporting Burgundy and not Louis. When finally I signed the treaty* with the new Duke of Burgundy† (his father recently having died‡) it was time for Warwick to take stock of himself and his 'power'. Soon he was to see his brother lose his position at court, and his sister's betrothal to my brother Clarence seemed in imminent danger. Too, there was no sign from me that I feared or dreaded his wrath.

Slighted—which had been my full intent—Warwick retired to Middleham Castle to sulk, his foreign policy in ruins, his pride battered, and I proceeded with my plan to marry my sister Margaret to the new Duke of Burgundy.

On August 12th, Elizabeth brought forth another daughter, Mary, who was christened at Windsor. And now did I find treachery in the Yorkist nest, a cuckoo which had masqueraded as an eagle: Clarence, my brother, stepped from my side and joined forces openly with Warwick, the wily Kingmaker now broiling his plans again, this time with my brother as his puppet. Shortly, with his daughter Isabel married to Clarence, Warwick hoped to gain strength by backing Clarence—who could be looked upon as my heir, I having but two daughters. However, the King's permission was necessary for such a union, and that I would not give; nor would I support the quest for a Papal dispensation which would be essential for the match, the two being cousins.

Who could blame me for keeping my thumb pressed upon those who swarmed for power? Indeed, fool would I have

* 1467.
† Charles the Bold, future husband of Edward IV's sister Margaret.
‡ The late Duke was Philip the Good, husband of Isabella of Portugal, granddaughter of John of Gaunt (Edward III's son).

been blandly to smile and allow that union which would have endangered my Crown and my daughters' future! Yet when I summoned Warwick to court afterward, he refused to obey, saying, "Never shall I come again to Council while all my mortal enemies, who are about the King's person, namely Lord Rivers the Treasurer, and Lord Scales and Lord Herbert and Sir John Wydville, remain there present!" Did he think I would dismiss all these, who were proving themselves able and loyal ministers, to replace them with he who had flaunted himself as power-behind-my-Throne in France, and behaved like a spoilt and grasping toddler? Events had swerved too widely from that beginning he and I had made together what felt like a lifetime's entirety before. If I felt some *tristesse* at the abandonment of our old camaraderie, I had but to remind myself that, had he truly desired only my gaining the Crown, he would not have behaved so badly after that event. Surely, had that been the entirety of his ambition, he would have retired sweetly to Middleham, content and satisfied?

"He would be King in your stead!" Elizabeth told me, cradling our new babe in her arms. "Always have I mistrusted those narrow black eyes of his—and that acquisitive stare! He is not normal—other men look at me in many ways, but none like Warwick! He does not possess any quality above avarice; he is evil, Sire. Beware of him!"

My Queen had never looked more radiant or more desirable, her gilt hair streaming free, her autumn-gold eyes glinting with anger, and tiny Mary clasped in her slender arms. Our second child and, loving Elizabeth as I did, it worried me not one mite that we had no son as yet. Not even when the Lancastrians, spurred by news of the breach between Kingmaker and King, rose in revolt in various parts of England. They were erratic and misbegotten revolts, and destined for failure, but they showed that there was still dissension and unrest in my Kingdom. Meanwhile, Warwick retired to Calais, where once he had been Captain, it seeming that rebellion would fade to naught.

Months passed, and March brought me another daughter, Cecily, named for my mother, but full summer brought ripe revolt in the North, to which I journeyed with men and arms for the purpose of quelling the insurrection. Elizabeth, meanwhile, was on progress, visiting Norwich amongst other places, she being accompanied by our three daughters.

And now it was time for Warwick's evil to spring upon us; he had been secretly plotting to return to England with a force of men to snatch my Crown from me and replace Mad Harry on the Throne, naming my brother Clarence as heir, Clarence having been secretly married to his daughter Isabel in direct contrariness to my will.

It was July, 1469, and that month taught me how fickle was London City. In my absence in the North, it flung wide its gates to the Kingmaker and his band, welcoming him as long-lost hero and, in my absence, it was as if I had never existed; as if there *was* no Crowned King of England.

THE ROSE QUEEN: 1469–1470

However firmly Edward had assured me he adored our three daughters, and was undismayed that we had no son as yet, I was sorely upset by the lack of a Prince. Despite having three Princesses, the people craved a Prince as heir, for what woman had ever ruled successfully alone—or even been given opportunity? The Empress Matilda's reign had been an abortion of misery and dissent (much like Mad Harry's womanish reign) and there was no precedent for a Queen Regnant. When fickle traitor Clarence (he whose hands had trembled at my Coronation) allowed himself to be named as heir by Warwick, they planning to take England for themselves, my lack of a son was an unbearable pain within me. Yet never one word of reproach from Edward, and how I loved him for it!

Events brought tragedy, for while my King was dealing with the Northern rebels, Warwick and false Clarence took London, finding that city as false as they to my husband. And then the vile rebels rooted out those whom Edward had told to hide themselves—my father, Lord Rivers, and my brother, Sir John, dragging them from their forest hide-out at Dean, bearing them to Kenilworth Castle, *and there beheading them both.* . . . The new Earl of Devon was captured in Somerset and beheaded by command of vile Warwick, and the new Earl of Pembroke, Lord Herbert, was similarly slain at Bristol—they all four loyal and faithful King's men. For me tears were not enough to mourn my father and brother and the others murdered, nor for my poor mother arrested on a charge of witchcraft and tried like any common felon. And while we wailed and grieved, my beloved spouse was rudely woken from his sleep at Olney by the Archbishop of York and a band of heavily-armed men, taken to Coventry and there imprisoned in Warwick Castle. It was now August, and never had there been a more wretched, tragic summer. Misery and heartbreak clasped me in their cruel embrace; misery seemed to flow about me as I walked; the faces of my beautiful daughters made me weep with despair for their fate. My father and brother dead, my mother tried. (Yet found innocent! This astonished me, for I had believed Warwick capable of the lowest cunning; he could well have bribed the jury and had my mother burnt as a witch, despite his awareness of her purity. If he sought to rid England of the Wydvilles, why submit my mother to a fair and just trial? Too, my brother Anthony escaped from his oppressors and was in sanctuary.)

And I was prisoner in the Tower, Warwick's victim, and given none but the merest of necessities to sustain me and my family. I struggled to keep serenity, but my mind persisted in asking: What will the Warlock do? Thrust Mad Harry back upon the Throne? Call Clarence King? *Murder my husband?* This last thought never failed to drench my body with icy sweat, and I would strive to maintain tranquillity when I longed to scream and rail and burst from my prison to join Edward in the Warlock's castle. . . .

Later, I would hear how Edward was removed in secret from Warwick to Middleham Castle in Wensleydale, from whence the Warlock expected him to summon Parliament without murmur. Secretly concocting his own plans, Edward gave all the appearance of meekness and obeyed. I who knew him so well could guess at the fury fomenting behind the placid façade he effected with which to trick the Warlock Warwick. And now London, which had risen to the usurper's banner, turned once more about, declaring for Edward, they pronouncing that the beheadings and the imprisonment of the King were more than they had bargained for. (Bitterness engulfed me. What had they expected of the usurper? Smiles and gifts? Their fickleness had killed my father and my brother and caused my mother humiliation and hurt. In future, however loudly or loyally the Londoners cried for my husband and myself, I swore I would never trust them again. *Never.*)

In June 1468 Edward's sister Margaret had left England to become wife to the new Duke of Burgundy,* and now that Duke, hearing of Edward's imprisonment, sent message to London and its citizens that if they supported Edward and remained faithful to the Yorkist cause, he would give them all available assistance. Charles of Burgundy, member of the

* See Historical Note 1.

League of the Common Weal, was no minor lordling to ignore and shortly London was calm again and, to all appearances still loyal to Edward. But a fool was stewing plans on the Scottish border, Humphrey Neville by name, leading a band of men whose aim was to murder my husband and restore Mad Harry to the Throne!

I had believed every evil of Warwick, yet now he refused to support the Neville insurrection, despite his kinship with its leader, and requested aid from the Commons to quell the rebels. The Commons, who fully believed as I did at that time that Warwick meant to make himself King, refused to aid him. The Kingmaker, to prove he had not intended to appropriate the Crown for himself, promptly freed Edward, took him to York, and then on to Pontefract where he stayed until autumn. Then, on seeing him freed and robust, the Commons granted Warwick the men he needed and the Neville rebellion was quashed, its leader beheaded in York.

But what liberty Edward had gained was in actuality minute. He was still in Warwick's clutches, and would have stayed there no doubt had not England grown eager to see its handsome Edward again. Gradually, such an eagerness grew, until no single man could have dealt with it. The cry was for Edward back upon his Throne, and there was talk of invasion by Charles of Burgundy to ensure this very act. Warwick, dismayed, agreed to allow Edward to return to London—if he promised to do all he was told. Edward, who was still mimicking an amiable, biddable man, smiled and said he would obey.

October saw the King's return to London, great ceremony having been prepared for him and, from my window, I heard the cries and chatter of gladness. Richard, my husband's brother, his usual solemnity vanished, accompanied Mountjoy, Buckingham, Arundel, Hastings, Essex, Northumberland and others to greet the King. The Mayor and his Aldermen, garbed in scarlet, were present; so were the London craftsmen, attired in blue. Edward rode with one thousand men, entering the city by way of Cheapside, having left Warwick's brother, the Archbishop of York, at Rickmansworth. No one could have mistaken the Londoners' mood! It was one of utter delight at the reinstating of their Sun King, and I, awaiting him in the Royal apartment in the Tower, experienced a joy which had long eluded me. I wore black, mourning for my father and my brother, yet knew a moment of longing to be garbed in rich blue or gold when Edward saw me again. However, I need not have feared he would find me uncomely in such weeds; we had been married for more than five years, but we were lovers still.

That night saw a reunion of such intensity and joy that it equalled our marriage eve. Edward looked paler, and lack of activity had added flesh to his slender frame, yet there was no suggestion of his having lost either vitality or confidence during his imprisonment. Spilling his plans to me, he told me of the meek act he had upheld to dupe Warwick and his brother the Archbishop, they having been fooled totally by it. Delight sparkled in his eyes as he said that on the morrow the Earl of Oxford and the Archbishop were preparing to travel to London to join him.

"They think to have me, little dove!" he cried. "But they are fools to think me quiescent after all I have endured at their hands! They will begin their journey, yes, but a messenger will intercept them on their way and they shall be told to return to their lodgings and await my command! In truth, I vow I should vomit if I saw their nauseous faces again!" His face darkened. "I shall not—cannot—forget why you wear mourning, my love! However much they hated your family, or believed my advisers to be corrupt, they had no right to take the law into their own grasp!" Seeing tears flood my eyes, he pulled me close to him, the warmth and strength of his body reviving me.

"I am here now to protect you, and our daughters. Whatever Warwick planned before this day I think he knows his hour is done. London remembers my quest for peace before the Kingmaker brought dissension and distrust to England with him. By his very policy of bloodshed and execution, he has strengthened my Throne and assured my popularity with the people."

"You have ever been loved," I whispered, yet memory of London's recent disloyalty urged me to speak. "How can we ever trust this city again, Sire? England loves you, and now the Londoners cheer you—but only weeks ago they cheered Warwick. Who can say they will not turn again from you?"

Edward tilted my face to his. "I think they have learnt

their lesson. From what I have heard, it seems London welcomed the Kingmaker as a hero—remembering his part in my accession to the Throne—and were eager to show they still favoured him despite his rift with me. They had no idea of the holocaust that would follow his welcome—and they have eaten overmuch of Kings in prison and bloody battles. Now they sicken of it, and cry for their rightful King."

I let him comfort me, for to have spoken further of my doubts would have been to display lack of faith in his ability. But I would never know true ease in London from that day; always I would be waiting for it to turn traitor again.

* * *

Edward's policy was a placatory one, he continuing to smile blandly and appear biddable. With Warwick and his followers ever on the horizon, and disloyalty's memory uppermost in his mind, this was essential. Even vile, wine-swilling Clarence was included in the policy of friendship—much to my disgust. Yet I was able to quell my disgust at such things as these when Anthony, my brother, was brought back to court, he now taking our father's title of Earl Rivers. How good it was to see him again! And likewise my brother-in-law, quiet yet loyal Richard, Duke of Gloucester, who had never faltered in his support of our cause. He was made Constable of England and Chief Justice of North Wales.

Then followed the weeks of pacification, when Edward was at his most charming and amiable—yet never giving the appearance of weakness or stupidity. He has a gift for good-natured Kingliness at which I never cease to marvel, and now committed this gift to England's future. Yet there could be no rest while Warwick and Clarence were free, and fresh troubles in Wales—because of Gloucester's new title—prompted Edward to summon the Kingmaker and his son-in-law to court. A Grand Council was arranged for November, at which all peers must be present, Warwick and Clarence promising to attend. However, they failed to arrive until very much later, and then Warwick was bent on hostility and the brewing of discord. My family, Warwick told the Council insolently, was corrupt and immoral; they had deceived and tricked the Kingdom, appropriating money at every turn, and were enriching themselves at the country's expense!

Furious, Edward spat denial of this appalling accusation, yet for England's sake knew he must maintain some semblance of amity with the evil Earl. Swallowing his desire to have Warwick flung into the Tower, he begged for goodwill between all the factions involved in the disputes now disrupting his Kingdom, and in this Parliament was eager to assist. Warwick, they said, must recognise Edward as true King and obey him; and my husband must issue pardon—enforceable until Yuletide—to all those who had fought against him. So, for the sake of peace, the traitors were free, and unpunished, and my husband must control the overriding desire within him to have the rebels taken and executed. I too desired their execution, and had I been King I doubt whether I could have managed Edward's superb control. Never had I thought him more noble, or more lovable than at this juncture! When I found myself pregnant again, I was confident it was with England's heir. How could God deprive such nobility and sacrifice as Edward's of a son?

I too was asked to make sacrifice. My lovely Elizabeth, now four years old and as beautiful as a sunburst, must be betrothed to the son of Sir John Neville, Lord Montagu, the son, George, being created Duke of Bedford. This Montagu, hated Warwick's brother, would see his son married to England's fairest Princess, with every hope of that son one day becoming King of England—should I prove incapable of bearing a Prince!

Small wonder that I fumed, and was determined that the child I now bore would be a boy. See Warwick's nephew King of England? *Never!*

Because Warwick must be cosseted, so must Louis of France, and with this in mind Edward asked for French ambassadors to visit us. Louis—totally perplexed, no doubt—and believing Warwick and my husband to be amicable once more, prevaricated.

Meanwhile, the Earl and his *mignon* Clarence grew in confidence, thinking that England's disunity meant their security. Scrabbling around and about them, they built up their *cotillon* of followers, low, wretched turncoats all. Then, from Lincolnshire and Norfolk, came appalling news of feuding and bitter dispute between various parties. Our enemies were to make good use of this disruption!

There lived in Norfolk a troublesome, rebellious family named Paston whose feuds were notorious. Now they were at loggerheads with the Duke of Norfolk himself, causing him to retaliate strongly. And, simultaneously, battle developed between Lord Berkeley and the Countess of Shrewsbury. (Surely Mars is in the ascendant in their charts?) Then, whilst they growled and snapped at one another like table hounds scuffling for a discarded bone, Richard, Lord Welles, and his son—Lancastrians both—quarrelled with Sir Thomas Burgh of Gainsborough, Master of the King's Horse. Immediately Edward was alert, for Lord Welles's brother-in-law was Sir Thomas Dymmock, King's Champion, and he had allied himself with Welles against Sir Thomas. Edward had no recourse but to listen patiently to each side of the tale, assuring the men that he would give their feud his every concern.

All would have dwindled to naught had not Warwick snatched this chance to advance his cause and damage the King's. Despatching his spies amidst Lincolnshire people, he spread rumours of the King's impending retribution upon that county—which was, he spouted, to take the form of a vast army determined to crush the inhabitants, steal their property and possessions, and arrange mass executions. Panic swarmed, and the uprising which Warwick led from his own castle had many supporters, including the aggrieved Lord Welles. However, Edward again summoned Welles and his son to London, which interrupted their approaching rebellion, and to London they came, actually reaching Westminster, and there, knees knocking and faces blanched, they scampered into sanctuary at the Abbey. Eventually, chastened and humble, they came into Edward's presence and were pardoned after admitting their guilt. Thus Warwick lost himself a strong supporter, but the rumours he had flung about were bearing foul fruit and now the Lincolnshire commons rose against the Crown.

At Grantham, on March 12th, Edward had arranged to meet his army and his cousin Warwick to dispel the Lincolnshire rebels but, shortly before he took horse for this rendezvous, news was brought him of Clarence's proximity. And then my darling husband, softened by family love—which ever ruled him—agreed to meet wretched Clarence, they coming together in Baynard's Castle, under the haughty eye of Proud Cis, ever watchful of her brood. It was all effected before I knew; before I could cry "Caution! Beware!" to trusting Edward. As if they had never shared an ill word, my husband and his brother rode through the London streets from Proud Cis's home near Blackfriars Bridge to St Paul's, where they entered the church to pray together.

Later, Edward told me how Clarence had begged for Royal support for Welles's cause, attempting to delay Edward on his journey to Lincolnshire. He had engaged every trick to persuade him: smiles; flattery; promises of his ardent loyalty in future days; strenuous apologies for his past misdemeanours. Fond yet firm, Edward had managed to extricate himself from his brother's wiles without having made any damning promises and yet without having offended the capricious Clarence. A monstrous task in itself to one so family-devoted as he.

But nothing would placate Proud Cis's wolf cub. Having left his King, he scurried to Welles's side, holding conference with him and the Prior of St John's,* then departing to rejoin Warwick. At this time he was no more than a harlot who had offered his body to the highest bidder, forsaking family and love for the chilly embrace of Avarice. Had I known what he was about at that time, I think I could have killed him myself had he and I and a dagger come within inches of one another!

Welles, who had been generously pardoned, proceeded to summon men to his, Warwick's and Clarence's banners, they grouping in Yorkshire and Lincolnshire and thereabouts, their intent to rise against my husband in unlawful rebellion.

Edward, who had been expecting Warwick and Clarence to join him as ordered, withdrew this command on learning of Welles's action. However, a letter arrived couched in sweet familial terms: it was from Clarence, he so calming Edward's apprehension that Edward reissued his order for the men to assemble. Yet it was with caution, for Welles was now calling himself Grand Captain of the Commonalty of

* Langstruther.

Lincoln, he prancing about like a highborn Prince. Further orders were issued: Welles and Sir Thomas, the King's Champion, must leave London immediately and give full answer to their King. This they did, joining Edward at Huntingdon, where they appeared full laden with contrition, admitting their guilt in the uprising and in the misdirection of the people.

Their obedience—which had seemed courageous—was soon proved shoddy, for they had believed their earlier pardon would cover their fresh-shed crimes. It did not, of course, and both men were made captives, they being conveyed with the Royal party to Fotheringay. Now a hillock of cowardice, Welles managed to despatch word of his plight to his son Robert who immediately made plans to scamper to his rescue, intending to deliver him by moonlight's beneficence.

Edward, having left Fotheringay, had news of Clarence and Warwick, they saying they would join him within the day in Leicester; but there was naught to hear of Robert Welles until the Royal spies spilled the news of his organising a battle force within a few miles of Stamford where the King now rested. From this point—Empingham—Robert Welles planned to rescue his father.

Edward had behaved with honour and compassion; his enemies had not. Lord Welles was fully aware he risked execution if his son rose against the King; too, he knew that Sir Thomas faced a like fate. The King's patience had been callously employed against his Royal self, but now he acted, swiftly, decisively, and Welles and Sir Thomas were slain, and the Royal army on the march within a very short time, its objective Robert Welles and his gaggle of traitors.

To this day, the place where the combatants met is called Bloody Oaks, for great was the slaughter, the would-be traitors being put to flight or left for dead. The Royal cannon surprised them in their lair, and so mazed were they that they fled, ripping off their coats as they went, endowing the combat with the name of the Battle of the Lose-Coat Field. Truly did they strip off honour and virtue along with their jackets! Their foul leader, Sir Robert, fled as hastily as his men, leaving behind him the bodies of some of his slain officers, and one of Clarence's men, on whose body were discovered papers spilling every detail of an assassination plot, its victim my beloved husband.

I have often imagined Edward at the cessation of the Battle of Lose-Coats holding in his strong and beautiful hands the papers which revealed his brother and his cousin to be the lowest of hypocrites, the foulest of knaves. Despite all he had done in actuality, Warwick had ever pronounced himself active for England's good, his deeds necessary for its benefit, his support fully the King's, if not the King's ministers'. Misguided though his cousin was, Edward had attempted to see his side to the tale and keep peace with him. Now the truth was flaming like a beacon before him : Clarence was no young hothead to be forgiven repeatedly until he had internalised those lessons in life which would bring him back to the Royal fold. He was an unnatural brother : one who was avidly plotting the King's death with the King's own cousin, in the hope that he would be given the Crown. Knowing how devoted Edward was to all his family, tears would ever press behind my lids when I thought of that moment he learned the crushing truth. Had he been an arrogant or callous brother, or a vicious King, there might have been cause for Clarence's perfidy; as it was, plainly he was activated by murderous greed. Nor could it be said Warwick had led him astray; even when absent from the Earl's side, he had behaved with a full quiver of cunning, as at Baynard's Castle. Proud Cis had birthed a viper in George, Duke of Clarence. No wonder she rarely showed her face these days!

I had not thought to experience a moment when I would gladly relinquish all I possessed to be given oblivion's respite. On the field of the Battle of Lose-Coats, I knew that moment and was flung into deepest gloom.

It was then I realised how I had cosseted hope of my brother George's repentance, making excuses for his every disturbing act, calling him innocent and misled where I should have called him foul and savage. What cause had he to hate me so greatly that he could eagerly plot my death, and that whilst proclaiming loyalty to my very face? March's winds tossed my hair, yet it was more than the breeze which chilled my body, making every bone seem carved from ice. My parents had created a changeling in George, a monster shrouded by human flesh and human charm and therefore all the more dangerous. Memories flitted through my mind: George, red-cheeked with glowing eyes, making obeisance to me, his new King. George, attendant upon my precious Elizabeth, his expression rapt, his manner deeply courteous. George, vowing he had never meant me harm: could never mean me harm.

"Sire—dear brother—be ever assured of my loyalty to you," he had said at Baynard's Castle, his eyes clear, his brow unmarked. "Whatever ill you may hear of me 'tis only the concoction of our enemies! I work for your good, Sire! And ever shall! Believe me. . . ." He had pressed my arm with his fingers, looking directly into my eyes, and I had thought: How like our mother he is; the same mouth, the same eyes. And, thinking it, had been swept into trusting him. I should have recalled that the lips and eyes which make a woman beauteous make a man weak. . . .

"Brother," I had replied, "likewise be assured that should you hear I intend you any harm, then that, too, is the fabrication of our enemies. There will always be opportunity for you to speak your case to me; you shall not be condemned without that opportunity being given you."

And with that he had seemed content; for which I had

thanked the Saints. I thanked them too for the unswerving loyalty which the remainder of my family had given me: Richard, studious yet ever ready to do battle in our cause; Margaret, married to Burgundy, and equally as ready to provide Burgundy's support when I required it; Anne, wed to Norfolk, a valiant couple; Elizabeth, married to Suffolk, they equally mine. How different they from the feuding sons of Henry II and Edward III!

Yet, much as they loved me, their fidelity could not erase the pain brought me by George's lust for my death. (He had said, "*Sire, be assured of my loyalty to you,*" and "*Whatever you hear of me 'tis only the concoction of our enemies,*" and now in my hands lay documents detailing my own death, planned by my brother and my cousin. How dark and foul the world had suddenly become....)

I came back from my thoughts to find my men eager for departure. They had fought well, and the battle was ours. Now they needed warmth and wine and meat. (And yet had I lain wrapped in furs, with Hippocras and baked swan at my right hand, they could not have shielded me from the pain of my beloved brother's betrayal....) Stirring, I saw a corpse not far from where I stood, its head mangled and bloody from the assault of a flail, the hands leprous-white claws dug deep into the earth as if to dredge strength from it. Away to its right lay more corpses, globules of crimson beading their flesh; one, whose throat had been sliced in half had bled to death and now lay on his own scarlet carpet. Others, dismembered by the cannons, were strewn about, limbless, headless; and here and there lay a winter jacket torn from a back to assist a man's flight.

My own brother would have me slain like this, leaving me bloody, dismembered, lifeless, and then what of my Elizabeth and our sweet daughters? What of little Elizabeth's claim to the Crown? I saw George in my mind's eye, flushed and elated and smelling of malvoesie,* his favourite wine, the Crown of England on his head, my eldest child pale and sad locked deep in the Tower, my precious wife garbed in the mourning she hated, with Warwick appropriating all her possessions, her lands, her jewels, and George snatching at them to provide himself with the luxuries he cherished: the

* Malmsey, wine from Malvasia in the Morea of Greece.

furs, the gems, the wine (perhaps, most of all, the wine; he has ever drunk deep of it and to wildness-point).

Elizabeth had warned me many times of trusting a man because he is my brother, for she knows my weaknesses. I should have heeded her before; should have arrested George at Baynard's Castle and had him placed in the Tower. When he wed Warwick's daughter without my consent he wrote telling me how he loved her, and could not have borne another hour without her love; he said I had suffered similarly from love of my Queen, so should understand, and forgive. And, foolishly, I had, though my Queen spoke of the day England would see King Clarence upon the Throne, Warwick's daughter his Queen. I had listened, but not acted. And now the Warlock and his son-in-law were easing poisoned daggers into my heart.

When we had recovered from combat and were back in Stamford, I despatched orders to the plotters telling them to disband their armies and join me accompanied by the smallest number of outriders, as we had enjoyed victory against Robert Welles's men and an army would no longer be needed. My message gave them no clue that I had uncovered their plot, yet somehow word must have reached them for immediately they marched from Coventry to Burton-on-Trent with great defiance. (Could I have expected aught else of them?)

Welles's defeat was followed by insurrection from another segment of Yorkshire, its leader Lord Scrope of Bolton. There, men were complaining that Royal pardons were mockery, for Lord Welles and Sir Thomas had been executed despite theirs, and now must come danger to every life if such was the case.

We marched again, this time to Grantham where I gave orders to Northumberland to quell the rebellion. And, relieved of that task, I questioned Robert Welles and one of his officers who had been captured. They spilled a discordant, wretched tale of Warwick's plans to murder me and have George enthroned in my place; of Warwick's complicity in the Lincolnshire rebellion. But I was ice now, and hardened against my brother's ambition. Spies told me he and the Earl were making for Chesterfield and Derby with every intention, so it seemed, of strengthening the Yorkshire insurrection.

Having arrived in Doncaster, I sent out a herald with a message to the Earl and my brother this time letting them know I had proof of their assassination plot. They were to ride to my side immediately. (Weakness drowning me at the last moment, memory of George's eyes and mouth so like our mother's, I offered him full pardon would he but confess and seek forgiveness from me.) After, I cursed myself; I should put Elizabeth first, quashing that dangerous affection for my changeling brother.

Answer came from the two rebels. They would indeed do as I ordered, prostrating themselves penitently before me, but they feared the Queen's murderous relatives and desired a safe-conduct from me before they would venture one step; too, they required full pardon for all who were involved with them in their plans.

Anger replaced grief. Again, their talk of the 'murderous Wydvilles' suggested I was a weakly puppet King who allowed felons and criminals to thrive at my court. We live in harsh and bloody times, and surely they—Warwick and Clarence—were savage and bloody as any who lived? Their pretence at fear of 'murderers' sickened me.

It was mid March, and I ordered them to be at my side by the 27th. Soon after, Robert Welles was executed at Doncaster, my cousin and my brother were publicly pronounced traitors, and I led my men to Chesterfield at rapid speed. On reaching Rotherham, it was to find the traitors fled again, this time their plan being to enrol the help of Lord Stanley in their fight against me (they intending to take York and quell me and my force when we reached there). This time I did not follow them, the pursuit seeming fruitless and a wasting of energies. Soon, word was brought me of Northumberland's success in Yorkshire—a complete victory—he having conquered the unruly Northmen and even now their leaders—Lord Scrope and Robin of Redesdale*—were on their way to beg Royal pardon of me, each declaring that Warwick and Clarence were instigators of the Yorkshire uprisings.

* Believed to be Sir John Conyers, related by marriage to the Earl of Northumberland.

The North and its rugged, resolute men being lost to Warwick he abandoned them. I, being stronger both in force and followers than for a great while hitherto, marched determinedly to York and there heard the pleas of Robin of Redesdale who appeared to be the hero of all Yorkshire men. Too, I held audience with Northumberland who, though defeating the North in my name, nevertheless found subtle fault with me. He was a Neville and they were compiled of trickery and deceit, ever greedy and lustful for power and position. There was much rumour of his having supported Warwick at various stages of his conniving, or having planned to defect should my cause have been quashed. So, courting safety, I took from Northumberland his title of Earl, bestowing upon him in its place that of Marquis of Montagu, a paltry appendage, and, should he have hopes of becoming Earl again at later date, I had Henry Percy freed from the Tower—he being true Earl of Northumberland—allowing him the return of his inheritance. In return, Percy vowed loyalty to me and made gift of £8,000. We both were satisfied.

Meanwhile, I once more pronounced my brother and cousin criminals against the Crown, stripping my brother of his post as Ireland's Lieutenant and naming the Constable of England, implacable Worcester, his successor. This Earl, unrelenting and pitiless, was given full power to repel the rebels should they attempt to reach Ireland.

Now it was due time to make pause; we had marched, tramped and done battle without rest for what seemed like a ten year, the men were aching, weary, stiff of joint and grim of mind. But for me, with traitor-brother and rebel-cousin loose in the land there could be no complete relaxation, no freedom from apprehension. Cheated of Ireland, and of Calais, safe across the Channel, where loyal Wenlock was Commander, the traitors would leap for some city or county which they felt would support or aid them; which would it be? Soon, I heard : Devonshire.

Having reached Exeter, they scurried to Dartmouth where their spouses joined them, and from there they took craft to Calais, braving both April's rough elements and Wenlock's temper. Having made port at Calais, they found they were not welcome, which fact greatly surprised them

—but not myself—on hearing of it! However, it was not Wenlock who rebuffed them. Duras and Vaucler, deputy commander and chief of the port defences insisted the ship of traitors leave their shores. The merchants and traders of Calais, on whom the port depended, had need of my favour to continue their career of enrichment, and, at this juncture, Warwick and his band threatened their very existence.

Unable to believe the port which had once fêted him as its Captain would forbid him entry, Warwick's craft lolled in the harbour for some days—and there Warwick's daughter birthed a dead son : my nephew. For the child's burial, Calais opened its gates after much pleading on the rebels' part. And that was all; no doubt my brother and his Neville wife would think of Calais with small affection for ever more. Stranded at sea; a child lost—doubtless because of the harrowing events through which the Duchess had been pressed by her impetuous and avaricious husband; and once-doting Calais now chilly as a tomb. Shortly, much disillusioned, the ship of traitors headed for Normandy, landing at Honfleur on May Day, and there Warwick besought the aid of Louis the Spider King.

THE SPIDER, THE WARLOCK AND THE VIXEN: 1st MAY 1470–13th SEPT. 1470

No wilier intriguer than Louis XI* had ever eased his rump upon the Throne of France. Physically, an abortion of nature, his legs knobbly twigs, his head wide and overlarge, his manner of locomotion resembling that of a sot, yet possessed of a mind both unscrupulous and intricate as a bees' hive, the Spider King had toiled without pause since his accession in 1461, working to strengthen his country and his Crown. His father, Charles VII, who had begun his reign in a thicket of quandaries, doubts and anxiety, had progressed into the lactescent arms of the brilliant and beautiful Agnes Sorel, a creature as shrewd as she was dominant.

Briefly, at the beginning, there had been promise and hope, for Jeanne la Pucelle, the Maid of Orleans had incised the tremulous Charles with her vigour and her supreme optimism. However, after her burning, Charles's doubts and preoccupations recurred: his mother, the harlot Ysabeau of Bavaria had bedded with innumerable men: was he, therefore, of the Blood Royal of France, or the son of some lecherous Palace servant lured into the Queen's bed? He would never know, and this one doubt festered in his mind like a growth, swelling in size and sending out antennae which strangled his tranquillity and his talents. He inherited a Kingdom which, in St Louis' day, had been of purest gold but now was rotted wood bedevilled by woodworm and hung with tawdry tinsel where once there had been lustrous gems and chains of goldsmiths' work. The Hundred Years War with England and the horror and decimation of the Black Death† had bankrupted France, leeching it of optimism, gold, energy and order. The serene days of Philippe le Bel were but a halcyon memory: then, men had worked for peace and enrichment, gaining both, and Philippe had accrued all those items necessary for a

* See Historical Note 2.

† This was not in actual fact named the Black Death until more recent times.

country's continued prosperity, both moral and monetary: gold, power, respect, a workable system of Law, success, and pride of achievement. After him had reigned his three sons, Louis le Hutin, the Quarrelsome, Philip V, le Long, and Charles IV, le Bel. Not one of these three had sired a living son, and the Law of the Salic Franks* forbade that their daughters inherit. By 1328, the direct line of Kings from Hugh Capet was ended, and the first Valois, Philip VI, was King in French eyes. However, Philippe le Bel had married his daughter, the gilt-haired Isabella, to Edward Second of England and, in English eyes, their son Edward Third became King of France (the English not recognising the Salic Law). Had Edward Third been less determined, acquisitive and rapacious, there would have been little cause for anxiety, but he was all three. And so had begun the Hundred Years War which had depleted and malnourished England and France, rending and destroying them both piece by piece until only bloody fragments remained—fragments which would be bonded together again slowly by Louis the Spider in France and by the House of York in England.

But not without further disorder. Countries where the vicious and the vulpine have prospered and thrived for decades cannot become Elysian overnight. The redemption of France depended upon its King being more cunning and unscrupulous than any of his countrymen; the redemption of England depended upon its King being admired and loved—or at least respected—by every faction in that land.

France had given England three Princesses whose beauty was legendary in their own lifetime. Catherine de Valois,† bride of Henry V, and mother of Henry the Monk; Margaret of Anjou, his bride; and, before Catherine, there had been Isabella the Fair, wife of Edward Second. Three beauties who had altered the course of English history, Isabella by intriguing against her homosexual husband and allowing her lover Mortimer to plot his death, her son Edward Third becoming King. Catherine who had borne Henry VI, been widowed when he was an infant, and had taken Owen

* See Historical Note 3.

† It was written of her that "the beauty of her bosom deprived of reason all those fortunate enough to gaze upon it."

Tudor to her bed.* And now Margaret, with hair as jetty and lustrous as new-mined coals and a determination that was, at times, eerily inhuman. Louis the Spider knew full well that she, like him, had a nickname in England: there, she was called 'the Vixen' by the English who found aggressive Queens repellent but cherished those who displayed passivity and virtue. He knew too that she resembled him in many ways; they both were unscrupulous at gaining the prize they desired; they both schemed and plotted and intrigued, such pastimes being as nourishing as wine and meat to them. Perhaps their greatest disparity was their appearance, he being twisted and rachitic, she being voluptuous ivory and ebony. Yet Louis had no illusion about his goblin-like appearance. Inside his repulsively large head there lurked a brilliant and exceptional mind and had he the choice between mind and handsome form he would have chosen to retain the mind.

Secretly, he believed beauty to be a bar to efficient sovereignty. True, St Louis† had been extremely handsome but then God had been upon his side and he need not fear man. His Valois descendant believed beauty alienated those in proximity to the King—those who already envied him for his title and his Crown. Men could accept that their King inherited his status by birthright, but if he was also handsome and charming and successful with women—particularly the wives of his subjects—there lay disaster. Such a King was Edward IV who, Louis was told, had cuckolded a magnitude of his own subjects! (A man, returning home, business problems fretting at his mind, was scarcely liable to leap with joy at discovering his wife abed with his King—or recently risen from bedding with him—or contemplating that probability. A common lover could be set upon, punched about the head and flung, perhaps, into the Fleet but one's King could not be beaten or reviled. This was one of the reasons why Louis believed Edward IV would not remain secure upon his Throne for many more years.‡)

* From Catherine and Owen Tudor devolved the Tudor Royal Family.

† King Louis IX, 1226–1270, a monarch of the Capet line.

‡ In actual fact, Edward's popularity with the merchants' wives of London ensured his continuing success, proving that wives have dominance, even over cuckolded husbands!

It was May, 1470, when the King of England's greatest enemy landed at Honfleur in Normandy accompanied by the King of England's greedy and unruly brother, Clarence.

Louis, who had been bemused in the past regarding Warwick's true standing in England, was no longer thus. He knew now that the Earl was Edward's rival and antagonist, the gauze of alliance which had joined them having been ripped to shreds forcibly by each man. So, despite the Burgundians' desire—which was that their Duke's brother-in-law should not be enraged by having his foes welcomed in France—Louis despatched no less than an Archbishop and the Admiral of France to greet the rebel band. And shortly Louis received a gratifying message. It appeared that the Earl's immediate ambition was to pluck Edward of York from his Throne, there being no more pretence that Warwick abhorred the Wydvilles whilst supporting their Royal relative-by-marriage.

* * *

Reading the message, Louis was consumed by the most gratifying exhilaration. How many years had he waited to play his part in the destruction of the King of England? They had both acceded to their respective Thrones in 1461, Louis on the death of his father Charles VII, and Edward on the death of his father Edward of York and the deposition of the tremulous and vague Henry Six, that, perhaps, being the only similarity between them. As Dauphin, Louis had hungered to attack France, his motive hatred and contempt of his inept and lascivious father. However, when he became King, there was no longer need to destroy his parent or make assault upon his homeland and, aware that Christendom awaited his premier acts following his accession, Louis enjoyed a sensation of immense egotism. Gone was the Dauphin who had been exiled to Dauphiné by the King and in his place was the new King, omnipotent, revered, where before he had been slighted and misunderstood. His father's reign, as far as Louis was concerned, was an appalling disaster despite Charles's having been ably and loyally served by such as Jacques Coeur, Dammartin, the Bureau brothers, Richemont and Dunois, after he had summoned strength from Jeanne d'Arc with which to place himself upon the Throne. Posterity would pronounce his father 'Charles le Bien Servi'* and himself the Spider King (which to him was an infinitely preferable title, suggesting an immensity of genius for intrigue. And better by far than being called White Rose of Rouen as was Edward IV!). The new King of France proceeded to display an impulsiveness which he was to regret bitterly within a very few years, its result being the War of the Public Weal in 1465—which he had won, its existence having taught him a great deal about Kingship. Afterwards, he had courted diplomacy and tact—at least upon the surface. One of his earliest major acts, in 1462, had been to give his support to Margaret of Anjou after she had fled to France from England and, subsequently, Edward of England had given his support to Burgundy and Brittany. So, by various tactics, Louis had seduced the Earl of Warwick to his side, hoping in this way to strengthen that part of his web which he was busily spinning across the Channel and, at one time, there had been the possibility of a marriage between a French Princess and King Edward—which possibility had evaporated when Edward married Elizabeth Wydville. She, beautiful, intelligent and incredibly shrewd, was niece of the Count of St Pol,† who planned to assist Burgundy in its invasion of Picardy. . . . Then had come the War of the Public Weal, after which Louis had asserted his authority not only in Paris but in Brittany, where he had overpowered its Duke, only Burgundy then remaining a threat. But its Duke, Charles the Bold, was husband to Margaret, King Edward's sister, England standing staunchly behind the Dukedom as it stood behind England. Therefore, Charles, whose temper was mercurial and extremely violent, could afford to intimidate the Spider King—which he proceeded to do and, in 1468, Louis was compelled to agree to terms Charles sought, these including the passing of Champagne and Brie to Louis' brother, Charles of Berri (these places being convenient trade links between Burgundy and Flanders), and the gifting

* The Well Served.

† The Count of St Pol was Louis de Luxembourg, brother of Elizabeth Wydville's mother, Jacquetta.

of Louis' aid to the Duke in his fight to quash rebellion at Liège. (The Duke and Charles of Berri being great friends.)

However, agreement was as far as the terms progressed, for Louis had no wish to part with Champagne and Brie—duchies which had been brought to the French Crown by Jeanne, wife of Philippe le Bel. Instead, Charles of Berri found himself with Guienne—to which England laid claim. Thus the King's brother became England's opponent and thus opponent of the Duke of Burgundy despite their friendship and alliance during the War of the Public Weal.

This was the age of the human vulture, when country preyed upon country and feudal Lord upon his master. It had begun with Edward Third of England determined to claim France through his mother's line, and had ended with every lordling driven by ambition turning upon those who could, by being overpowered, enrich his coffers and his heritage. Philip VI, rightful King of France in French eyes, had been supported by Scotland, Bohemia, Flanders and the Pope; Edward Third by Philip's brother, Robert of Artois, the Flemings of Ypres, Ghent and Bruges, Bavaria and Brittany. And, along with the skirmishes and battles, the horror of the Black Death, the confusion and starvation, the rapine and plundering, had swarmed a malevolent hatred which, disaster by disaster, had developed into a beast no man could control, the English blaming all upon the French, the French upon the English. Such malice and malevolence could not be destroyed overnight, and indeed it seemed men wished to nurture this hostility, not cure it.

Only forty-seven years before, there had been the defeat at Crevant, when the English and Burgundians had beaten the Scots and the French. The following year—1424—the Scots and the French had been defeated at Verneuil, the English then invading Maine. Orléans, 1429, had been the scene of French despair and English supremacy when Jeanne d'Arc had begun her brief reign, invigorating the French and inspiring them with sufficient zeal to thrust the English from their dominant positions. Later, she had commanded the French at Troyes and Rheims, eventually persuading Louis' dilatory father to have himself crowned. But she could not push him farther. Long though she did to eject the English from Northern France, she was hampered by a procrastinating, tremulous monarch and by her own enemies, la Tremouille, and the Duke of Burgundy, who sold her to the English for ten thousand francs in 1430. Her death by burning left behind a legend of such magnitude that, even as she perished, an English soldier—and this the enemy—cried, "Heaven help us, we have burnt a Saint!"* Louis, who would have given his all for Jeanne to walk into his court, could never forgive the English for her brutal death, his father for so weakly allowing la Tremouille to plot the Maid's betrayal, or their indifference to her fate when she lay in the hands of the '*godons*'.†

After the Maid's burning, nothing had been the same. That contrition and devouring guilt which had claimed all those responsible for her death—except the unrepentant Charles and la Tremouille—had pervaded every part of France within a very short while. Soldiers, peasants, priests who had seen the burning or heard of it at first hand travelled back to their villages, their towns and hamlets, farms, châteaux, manors and castles, repeating the tale of Jeanne la Pucelle, who was surely a Saint, and who had been cruelly done to death by Satan's minions—the English.

Young Louis, seven when the Maid was burnt, grew up hearing her story repeatedly from friends and nursemaids. As he grew to manhood, the picture of her remembered from when she lived at court slowly faded—though it was replenished from time to time by others who remembered her more acutely than could a small boy. From his friends and companions—servants, too—he had never heard one suggestion that she was deserving of her fate, nor had anyone a critical word to speak against her. Even now when he was forty-seven, there remained in his mind a dim, sepia outline, slender, taut, asexual, the eyes almond-shaped and brilliant, the chin slightly receding, nose gently retroussé, mouth as rosebud-like as any courtesan's. He knew that the legend of Jeanne la Pucelle included the fact she had cropped her hair like a man's, thereby shocking prelates and clergy, yet he could recall her hair as extremely wavy—almost kinky—and he had never seen it cut shorter than

* See Historical Note 4.
† 'God-damns': French name for the English.

shoulder length.* Nor had anyone else; only those who lived abroad, or heard stories rendered inaccurate by repeated telling, would continue the fabrication of Jeanne's straight, Norman-like hairstyle. However, though the mind-picture was dim, Louis attributed no less an importance to the Maid. Though deeply supersitious and as godly as any of his countrymen, Louis possessed a mode of religion which allowed every facet of human—and inhuman—nature to take its place, so it was not a picture of Joan the Saint which drove him to abhorrence of the English. It was Joan the Soldier who had ejected the vile English invaders. This Joan was a national hero, a splendid, inspired creature who taught the English to fear the French, and then was burnt at the stake by her enemies after being betrayed by her own countrymen.

These facts, which frequently slipped through Louis' mind, rose again in full force after he had read the message from the Earl of Warwick. Playing the strenuous game of diplomacy, he had intrigued with the Earl to gain King Edward's hand for a French Princess. Then had come the rude rebuttal when Edward had married one of his own subjects and, following this, Louis found himself engorged with that hatred and bitterness which he experienced when thinking of those who had burnt la Pucelle. Later, Edward's forceful dethroning of Margaret of Anjou and her banishment from England had further swelled Louis' detestation of the man. Though secretly the former act had not unduly perturbed Louis, the latter did, and it was easy then to put the two acts together, seeing them as a gross insult to his country. Some might be prepared to forget, allowing the tragedies of the past to become no more than legends, but not the Spider King. . . . Forty years before, when his own father had not the courage to have himself crowned despite his being the rightful monarch, a young woman had inspired him with her courage, her determination and her forthrightness. And, because of that woman, Charles had become the seventh French King of that name at his coronation in Rheims and, in due time, because of this, it was

* I have taken this description after studying the only authentic drawing done of Joan of Arc during her lifetime. This was possibly by Clement de Fauquemberge, clerk to the Parlement of Paris.

possible for his son Louis to become Louis XI without there being any suggestion he was unfitted to reign. (If his father had remained uncrowned, God knew what his, Louis' fate would have been!) He owed much to la Pucelle whom the English had tried, pronounced guilty of sorcery and witchcraft, and burnt at the stake.

Hatred gushed through Louis, bubbling inside him, spewing itself through his rachitic and repulsive body. Hatred for all those humiliations and tragedies which the English had caused, and for Edward IV who had dethroned a French Queen of England, and repudiated a French Princess as his bride. Louis desired revenge, desperately! And now here was the Earl of Warwick and Edward IV's rebel brother, Clarence, landed upon his own shores, sending him messages conveying lust for the destruction of the King of England! What could be more fortuitous than this? For, with the Kingmaker's aid, not only could Edward of England be destroyed, but there was opportunity to replace him with a Frenchman . . . or woman. Louis strummed his bony fingers upon the armrests of his Throne, one eye half-closed—a habit of his when in thought. A French monarch upon the English Throne . . . perhaps his fiery cousin, daughter of his mother's brother? What of that cousin? Since being rudely ejected from England by the Yorkist King in 1461, she had fled to Scotland and from there to her father's court in Anjou. (If she had been confident of support from that source she was rudely disappointed, for her father, ageing and besotted with his young wife Jeanne de Laval, had smiled but shaken his head sadly. What strength did he possess these days? he told Margaret. How gladly he would have assisted had he the gold or the power, but her brother, the Duke of Calabria, had recently embarked upon one of his ventures—this time to Italy—and gold stores had been depleted to outfit him and his men. Sadly, there was not a coin left to help a deposed Queen regain her Throne. . . .)

So the Queen without a Throne, and her son Edward of Lancaster, began their crushing and humiliating search for a protector who would finance the redemption of their Crowns, eventually finding that there was no one in France who was prepared to aid them. Gradually, the Queen—Margaret of Anjou—sold her jewels and soon was existing on meagre gifts of money from her father. And it was then that Louis had invited her to his château at Amboise.

There she found him willing to finance her scheme, he advancing her 20,000 *livres* and the permission to gather a suitable army from those French knights who were willing *but only on condition she promised Calais to Louis.* Louis, who had doubted his cousin's right to the nickname of 'Vixen' given her by the Yorkists, was pleasantly pleased. Not only had she agreed to part with Calais, but she had needed little persuading. The 20,000 *livres* and two thousand soldiers had accompanied her to England, Pierre de Brézé as their commander.

The result had been the disastrous battle on the outskirts of Hexham Forest, the Lancastrians again being defeated, after which Margaret scurried deep into the Forest itself for sanctuary. There, de Brézé persuaded her to return to France, which she did, taking refuge with Philip of Burgundy (a man incredibly ancient for his times, he being all but seventy years of age).

The Truce of 1463 between France and England had forcibly quelled Margaret's hopes of receiving further assistance from Louis and so, accepting defeat, she had retired to the castle of Koeur near Verdun—a gift from her father—where she had remained to this day. As far as he, Louis, knew, she expended all her energies upon her son Edward, educating him as befitted a King—though there seemed little hope of his ever having a Crown. Until Pierre de Brézé's death, there had been great gossip of him and the Vixen bedding together, but then there had always been gossip of Margaret of Anjou and some man or other.

So who lay in Louis' web now? An English Earl devoured by need for revenge; Clarence, brother of the King of England, who was married to the daughter of the vengeful Earl; and the dethroned Lady of Anjou, still beautiful, still spirited, possessing a son who was rightful King of England in Lancastrian eyes—but above all *French*. How bring these four together, when the Earl had once assisted in the Lady's destruction? For, these four combined—together with himself—might very well be the means of bringing the English Throne to France.

How might he do it? Tempt the Earl by promising his

son-in-law the Crown of England, his daughter thereby becoming Queen? Maybe. Maybe. Tempt the Lady of Anjou by promise of the Crown of England for her son, the Regency for herself until his majority? Louis' eyes gleamed. When he held every advantage, there was nothing more gratifying than playing one against the other! The Earl, the Lady, and the Prince of Lancaster were landless and impoverished, and all were lusting for the English Throne, yet, at the moment, they were established enemies. Could he, by exercising those skills which were his very nature, bring them together, make them allies, allow each to believe his major ambition would be gained, and thereby bring himself the longed-for jewel, the glittering emerald of England? Patting the pouch hanging from the leathern belt at his hip, he heard the delicious clunking of gold from within it. Yes, impoverished and ambitious were those whose alliance could bring him England, and *he* possessed the gold which could enervate their cause. Too, he possessed the wit and acumen to juggle the avaricious puppets into every pose he desired until, when they had served his purpose, he could slice their strings with a neat, swift cut, leaving them floundering—devoid of life—upon the earth, impotent as mannikins flung aside in the toybox.

His lips curved into a malicious smile. His enemies called him Spider, saying he spun webs of intrigue and design to cripple all those who endangered his Crown lands, accusing him of cruelty more vicious than practised by any others even in these violent times (he had been condemned for allowing his soldiers free rein to torture and murder during his campaign in Switzerland), they putting about the tales that he had caused the death of his first wife, Margaret Stuart, by poisoning, had dealt similarly with his father's mistress, Agnès Sorel and had, by sorcery, murdered his father. However, all of it—except what had occurred in Switzerland—was malicious fable; yet, fable or not, it was attributed to him, and therefore he was labelled poisoner, wizard, necromancer, Satanist, for all time . . . which fact gave him little motive to be godly or circumspect. Label a hound malcontent, or vicious, and he will be thus and Louis had been granted generous rein to snap and scavenge, snarl and attack wherever he so wished it. . . .

Warwick had not long to wait for reply from the King of France, and the message when he received it filled him with elation. Not only was Louis amenable to the Earl's plan but he would render assistance to bring about the destruction of Edward of England. At first sight, the message appeared miraculous; at second rather too effusive and eager for sincerity. Biting upon his thumb, Warwick walked the floor of his cabin as restlessly as an insomniac. He had no liking for the ignominious role he was being forced to play by Destiny. By nature he was an adventurer, a lover of freedom, an opportunist and a fighter, being born under the sign of Sagittarius the Archer and therefore not taking easily to those who would attempt to master him. Oh, he could appear to assume a lowly role—that of Kingmaker and not King—but only on condition that the King remained subservient to his advice, recognising him as the more knowledgeable of the two. Pride playing a massive part in his life, he was basically a very unaccommodating person yet as long as those with whom he dealt acknowledged him their superior he was smugly content. When they escaped from his bigoted rule, as had Edward of York, he was forced to deal violently with them, having no other efficient method of manacling their discontent. This inability to adapt was his great weakness, yet he would have it as being his strength. His era, which was undergoing massive transformation and change, was no longer one in which the narrow could flourish beyond a certain point and, like the partner in a marriage who fails to realise his mate has developed—gaining different needs from those which brought them together—Warwick was facing disaster yet totally unaware of it.

Having ascended at incredible speed, he had switched loyalties like a questing bird seeking the most promising worm, had climbed upon the precipice of power, there to discover himself as unheeded by his protégé Edward as if he were non-existent, invisible. He had gripped power in his hands, had drunk it from jewelled goblets, and devoured it from platters of thick yellow gold, finding it an intoxicating diet, and as addictive as malvoesie or mead. But now his palms were empty, his platters and goblets likewise, and he was hungering more passionately for their contents than any man has ever hungered for meat or wine. . . . So ravenous was he that he was prepared to place himself beneath the wily thumb of Louis the Spider that he might regain the splendent and powerful position lost to him.

Tasting blood, he looked askance at his thumb to see he had bitten deep into its flesh without heeding the pain. Binding linen round the wound—but carelessly, as soldiers tend their wounds, thinking it womanish to dwell upon them—his narrow eyes fell upon the curling parchment bearing the seal of Louis XI. The man whose buttocks heated the Throne of France was known to be many things: vicious, grasping, unreliable, malevolent, yet still he remained an enigma.

"To trust . . . or suspect?" Warwick whispered, finding himself in vast need of one to advise him as he had advised others yet unaware that, even if that person existed, he would continue his own egotostical way nevertheless . . . being fulsomely guilty of that very arrogance which he had attributed to Margaret of Anjou and Edward of York.

"What will it be? Follow, where I love to lead? Or accept defeat?" No—even the thought of defeat made him physically ill. Then it must be to follow, meekly, with the subservient air of acquiescence which he abhorred, for Louis of France would not tolerate any other attitude in those he aided. Even if his men-at-arms returned with reasonable wealth from their *sortie* into Normandy—where they had gone today, like other days, in an effort to barter their war-spoils for coinage—that wealth would not be sufficient to finance the resurrection of the emblem of his House—the Bear and the Ragged Staff. For that, great wealth was needed and that available from a source which could provide more immediately it became necessary. To resurrect his emblem upon its bright banners in England, to place his own puppet-King upon England's Throne, to see his daughter Queen of that country one day, he would need Louis of France; of that there was little doubt.

Though the knowledge clutched him by the throat, constricting his pride as surely as a murderer's hands destroyed the life in him, he must go begging to the Spider King, bowing, flattering, cajoling, and all the while smiling like a pauper-woman at the feet of a Lord. He must. Yet the very act would crucify him....

THE VIXEN

She was forty, yet knew herself undrabbed by time, unmarred by deprivation. Aware she was dubbed Queen of Shades by her enemies, and vile harlot, too, she had sufficient resistance to repel the gibes, and the insults. After all, though she had lost a Throne and a Crown, and a weakling, timorous husband, she had a son, and he was handsome and healthy.

Edward was eighteen, and her universe. During the past few years of enforced exile, whilst struggling to live royally upon her father's pension of 2,000 *livres* per annum, Margaret would have collapsed many times if she had not had Edward to support and cheer, and to tutor in the ways of Kingship. For, despite their exile, and the vigorous Yorkist upon England's Throne, Margaret had never ceased to dream of that day when her own son would recline upon that Throne. Men died; men contracted diseases and were smitten overnight; men had riding accidents and Edward loved hunting when he was not in the dangerous thicket of the battlefield; men could be assassinated, brought to their knees by a dagger between their shoulder blades, or a draught of poison in their wine. Any one of these could happen to Edward Fourth, and daily she prayed one would, her prayers hissing from between her teeth, seeming to bear some vile poison of their own.

"Let him be slain, dear God! Brutally, vilely slain! Hacked and dismembered! Horses trampling his remains, his limbs cast in all directions with no priest to shrive him first!" she would cry. And, on days when hope evaporated a little, "Let scavenging crows swoop down as he rides, and gouge out his eyes with their beaks! Let him writhe and scream, be blinded and terrified, and let the gaping wounds absorb the vile humours in the air and suppurate—let them poison him from within! Let him die *screaming* with agony!"

The men she had cherished and trusted—her supporting

father-figures in a desperate world—had been slain because of Edward Fourth and his father before him. Her sweet Suffolk. Precious de Brézé, whom she had taken to her bed and with whom she had shared a passion all the more intense for its lateness in her life. Her Lords and advisers—men she had needed in place of the dominant husband Henry could never be—and who had been taken from her one by one. Had there been no Richard of York, no Edward of York, no fiendish turncoat Warwick, she would still be Queen of England, her son the Royal heir. As she thought upon this for the hundredth time, tremors coursed through her limbs, almost painful in their strength, and she gripped her hands together, looking down at her slender fingers. Once she had worn amethysts and diamonds upon her fingers, and pearls and rubies luscious as fruits, thick gold claws gripping the gems, these being first jewels of Anjou and then of England. But all had been sold in recent years to buy food and wine, a home for her son—and equipment and men-at-arms to fight Edward Fourth. It seemed it was in her stars to end her life in poverty, foolishly glad for morsels of charity flung her where once she had been a Royal monarch, supreme, omnipotent. Men were taught to pity beggars and give them alms and *largesse*, yet what sufferings compared with those of a monarch brought low, struggling to survive on a few meagre coins? Beggars were oblivious to the joys of wealth and power and could only surmise concerning the possession of these, their imaginations being as impoverished as their skeletal bodies.

The bitter, swelling rage which Margaret was experiencing would end with her lying weak and exhausted upon her bed, she knew that, being too familiar with this scalding, draining emotion. Finally, her head would pound as though she had been kicked about the ears, and her eyes would dim, she then seeing only blurred outlines when people approached her. Sometimes there would be the incandescence of dazzling lights to herald the pain; sometimes not. Those physicians whom she had consulted regarding these attacks had failed to inform her of their origin, or their cure. "Reaction to the noxious vapours inherent in the night air" had been one physician's verdict. "Over-consumption of rich and cloying foods," had been another's diagnosis. Yet another had declared the cause to be "the wearing of the Royal crown and the unwieldy weight of the Royal robes." Of old, the attacks had followed periods of excessive activity and energy; now, they were more frequent, appearing without warning except—upon occasion—for the blinding silvery lights. Her father had always said she was as nervous and taut as a young colt, and one physician had mentioned this tension as possible cause of her attacks. "Madame," he had said, "there are some who possess bodies as well-armoured as though they wear mail; and there are those whose bodies are as vulnerable as though they were without flesh. The first can repel fears and worries; the second absorb them like food and wine, the absorption brewing this malady which rises like mist from the lower extremities and upwards into the head. The result: agony, and all those symptoms which you have recounted to me."

Relieved, Margaret had ordered him to concoct a cure, and this he had attempted, mixing her a syrupy fluid which coated her tongue and throat, sickening her yet bringing some small surcease from pain. After consuming the syrup, it had rendered her strangely exhilarated and oblivious of care, and when facing some unpleasant or frightening occurrence—battle, or interview with an enemy—she had imbibed a goblet of it, welcoming the consequent elation and confidence. Now, exiled from London, she had no recourse to that physician, and therefore no means of obtaining the healing concoction. That, perhaps, was more cruel than the loss of her gems.

Edward, her son, seemed to care little for her attacks—or for any of her problems except those which affected him. She had reared him by spoiling and pampering; had treated him as a King from his cradle; had so suffused him with a sense of his own omnipotence that he now considered her beneath his attention. Yet she blamed the disruption and violence of their era more than anything for his callousness. Once, he had been rose-cheeked and rose-natured, a bright and smiling boy, affectionate and sweet, but Edward of York had put paid to that! By the time her son was eight—having absorbed a surfeit of violence and upset in that brief period—he possessed the hardness of a seasoned knight and, when questioned as to how a certain troublesome trinity of

Yorkist knights should be punished for their misdemeanours, he had said, firmly and coolly: "Behead them!" At which, one of the knights, Sir Thomas Kyriel, had murmured: "May the wrath of God fall upon those who have taught a child to speak such words!"

She should have known that a boy who can so turn against his enemies would one day turn against her. . . . Yet still he maintained a superficial respect for her—though not sufficient to content a woman as desperate for affection as René of Anjou's daughter. Henry, her bemused and confused husband, had been more affectionate in his more lucid moments!

But she must not think of *him*, for to do so would be to see dank prison walls, darkness and horror, these together evaporating what courage she had remaining. Sighing, and aware that she had but few moments before the pain in her head forced her to her bed and a darkened room, Margaret walked towards the nearest window. It was a narrow and dust-shrouded slit, for the servants here did as little work as possible. From it, she could see the minute court below, and her son—seventeen years of age and slender as a reed—walking with a book in his hand. As he turned at the far end of the court she saw his face, so like his father's in the refinement of its features and far too feminine for a man who would be King of England if God answered her entreaties. Henry her husband had not inherited his own father's leonine and firm-jawed face, nor his mother's beauty, having, instead, a narrow triangular face with pointed, jutting chin, and acquiline nose, his lips being tightly and prudishly compressed, his brows perpetually frowning, his eyes bleak yet cloudy. Her son had not the wasted structure of Henry's cheeks and chin, nor the miserable expression, but only the features which seemed to be etched thinly upon his face betraying what? weakness? Certainly not feebleness of mind! All she could recognise of herself in the boy was the sensual lower lip and the dimples at the mouth's corners. All else was—as her enemies repeatedly declared—the boy's Valois inheritance from his mad great grandsire, Charles VI of France.

But what was this? Had she become as weak as moon-fevered Charles that she agreed now with her own enemies?

Margaret was about to withdraw from the window when she saw the horseman, her eyes recognising the emblem of the Spider King upon his doublet as he approached the château. Shrinking into the shade of the window embrasure, she pressed her head into her hands, too assaulted by pain to hurry and greet the Royal messenger. The waiting and the despairing had all but finished her....

* * *

The boy born heir to Henry Six of England welcomed the Royal messenger alone, his face irradiated with delight, for any contact with Royalty or things Royal always incensed him with joy. He was starved of the pomp and power which had marked his infancy, the servants making reverent obeisances before him and his mother, the pageantry of colour and richness which accompanied Palace life, and the knowledge he was to be King of England next, his signature having been added to all Royal documents—along with that of his father—since he was seven years old. (The moonfever rampant in his father's mind which had necessitated the boy being brought into the public eye while he was still an infant was a shameful fact which Prince Edward chose to forget. His was the pride of the Plantagenets and of Anjou, deep, fervent, implacable; a pride which chose to conceal all that which was unpleasant or repulsive, even if this meant denouncing his own father in the process. This he had done, and was now in the act of rejecting his mother for she was infuriatingly content to bide in charity's limbo, incarcerated in this isolated château where she did little but mumble and whine about the day her husband and son were restored to their Crowns. Once, she had been active and ambitious; now she was like an old beldame . . . useless, crook-minded, chunnering of days past and glorious memories.) Privately, Prince Edward wondered how two such ineffectual, ill-starred people as his parents had sired such a handsome, courageous, strong-minded son as he. Never had he faltered or feared in battle, nor cringed when confronted by their Yorkist enemies. It had been his mother who had fled at signal of defeat or disaster, his mother who had coerced him into leaving England and taking refuge here in France where they had been more or less ignored by King Louis, much to Edward's disgust. Now—at long last—the King of France's own brightly-caparisoned herald was dismounting in the dingy courtyard of René of Anjou's humble château, and bowing respectfully before him, Edward, heir to England's Crown.

Anticipation glossing his face, the young Prince waited eagerly to hear the herald's message.

* * *

Margaret felt uneasy. Ever since Louis' herald had outlined the French King's plans to her she had experienced the most unsettling breviary of emotions, hope and exultation, succeeded by gloom and despair, which in their turn were succeeded by enervating optimism. All of which had proved to her she was not so content as she had believed in her château with her son and their few bedraggled servants. . . . Yet she knew Spider Louis of old—he was a trickster of the most mephitic brew, as evil and as unreliable as Satan himself. And Warwick, turncoat and traitor, was now in league with him!

It was June now, and she had kept Louis waiting for her decision since spring. Then, finally, her old impulsiveness had swarmed, beating down her doubts, and she had agreed to come to Amboise, his château upon the left bank of the Loire. Situated upon a slight elevation of rock, the château was, some said, built by the Romans—great warriors and conquerors—this, Margaret hoped, being a good omen for her success. Too, the château had once belonged to Hugh of Amboise who had enriched himself by accompanying William of Normandy to England in 1066—and Hugh was called 'the stem of that illustrious House of Amboise which won such renown for itself as to be called the race of Mars', she herself being born under the sign of Mars. Such comforting thoughts she gathered to herself hungrily, hoping by their presence to exclude her private terrors.

The château was airy and pleasant, with carved windows, peaked tourelles, and high chimneys. Its stables had been erected in the time of Louis Philippe, and its main quarters had been inhabited by soldiers until Louis the Spider's time

—for it had been a Royal fortress until Louis had it renovated for his second Queen, Charlotte of Savoy (who even now was resident here, and expected to give birth at any time). Charlotte was a handsome woman, sturdy and statuesque, with slightly proturberant yet glowing eyes, and a quality of facial bone-structure which Margaret deeply envied, that envy being translated by her into petty dislike. Louis himself treated his Queen with little respect, and they were quite content to live apart when the necessity arose. He had never been a womaniser, nor was like to become one.

René her father was here too and they had met and wept in one another's arms. Now it was time to meet the King and turncoat Warwick, and trepidation bubbled in Margaret's body.

Louis, when he entered the audience chamber was as she remembered him from childhood—skinny, misshapen, bulbous-headed, his body submerged in ill-fitting robes of dull brown,* and upon his huge head the hat bearing its many badges, one for every saint who took his fancy. And they not even gold! thought Margaret as the King approached. The badges were base metal, and she had seen similar ones on servants and even on beggars in the streets. . . . Then her mind was snatched from concern regarding the King's outfit, for, loping behind Louis, dark-visaged and displaying a humility utterly foreign to him, came Warwick, her dreaded enemy. Snakes of revulsion undulated across her flesh, even her scalp seeming to prickle. Beecause of this greedy Earl she, her son, and her husband were destitute and Throneless!

Louis advanced, a crooked smile hooking up the corners of his mouth, his very reverence towards her increasing her fears. He smiled, then bade her rise when she would make obeisance; he asked after her health, her son's; he spoke as if she would be fully reinstated in France, if not in England. Despite her suspicions, her delight grew and, when Louis presented Warwick, and the Earl fell to his knees before her, begging forgiveness for his perfidy and craving her mercy, power soared in her, trampling on her doubts. She was triumphant again, a sovereign, Royal cousin of the King of

* After seeing Louis XI in 1461, the citizens of Abbeville declared, "His horse and dress altogether are not worth 20 francs!"

France, and rightful Queen of England! And, swift upon that engulfing emotion came need to exercise it and this she did, making Warwick kneel before her for no less than a quarter hour while she rearranged her gown and tucked in a trio of errant jetty hairs which had escaped her headdress. Then, when she had gestured that the Earl might rise, she bade greeting to the other Earl present—Oxford—with much more show of friendliness. Suitably rebuffed, Warwick kept his meekness about him, yet still Margaret refrained from pronouncing she had forgiven his perfidy. Anxiously, seeing England slide from his fingers' grasp because of a foolish woman's pride, Louis gave voice to reassuring words.

"Madame, should you have great doubt of My Lord Earl's fidelity to your cause, I will vouch most willingly for him. Indeed, I promise most fervently that he will prove trustworthy!"

She should have said, "How can the worm who constantly turns judge the stability of those beside him?" but she was desperate now for want of England and her Crown—she even fancied she could smell England's emerald hedgerows and moist summer air upon the Earl's robes, and she sickened for sight of that verdant monarchy. So, before the words swarming in her throat were swallowed with her spittle, she let them fall from her lips, and saw the faces of those present lighten as if tapers had been lit before them.

"Aye, then it is agreed?" Warwick smiled, a self-congratulatory leer.

But she held up her head to block Warwick's hasty assumption. "Nay, my Lord, not quite agreed. . . . You have been eager of late to cast filth upon my name and upon my son's name. Indeed, we have been called all number of vile titles at your behest, and with your support."

"Madame . . . !" began Warwick, but she interrupted him again, delighting at sight of his discomfiture. How he abhorred being reprimanded!

"So, My Lord, there must be earnest promise upon your behalf that there shall be no more of this. Should I hear to the contrary regarding your opinions of me, my anger shall be mortal and its victim *you*. . . ." Those present, who had been inclined to dismiss the Princess of Anjou as old and drained of spirit, recognised the indomitable Margaret who had rent England apart with her martial determination, such being the malice flashing from her eyes that even Louis stepped back a pace as though her tongue dripped venom. The outstretched hand which she had raised pointed first to one and then to another until she had included every man present.

Louis, eyes narrowed, realised that René of Anjou's daughter was as vituperative as ever. Yet what had he expected? That poverty and grief had acted upon her like palliatives, neutralising the acid in her nature? That surely would have been a miracle! Everywhere he turned he was surrounded by awkward and infuriating women. All his life he had been plagued by them! His mother, Marie of Anjou, had courted the conventual life, praying and making pilgrimages so frequently that often it seemed to her son as if she had barely returned from one before setting out on another. It had been her absorption with religion which had caused much of Louis' cynicism. And then there had been the appalling disaster of his first marriage to Margaret of Scotland, which had been arranged by his father when he was five and Margaret three and a half years old. They had been married at Tours in 1436, when Louis was thirteen, and he had disliked the Scots Princess from the first second of their meeting. Dreamy, vague, and desperately missing her family, she had trembled and wept almost constantly. Louis' father had responded by pampering her with gifts and gems, toys and pets to entertain her. Louis, sulky and resentful, found himself crushed by jealousy and distaste for the Princess who allowed herself to be so pampered. There was no plan for the marriage to be consummated immediately, as the Princess was too young; instead, she was kept beside Queen Marie for two years, during which time the spoiling continued, reaching an even greater magnitude after Margaret's father was brutally murdered, this causing her an excess of distress. Louis reacted by becoming deeply embroiled in his duties as Dauphin—which from that time were to take precedence in his life—and, shortly, ambition had gripped him to the exclusion of all else. Margaret, who revered the romantic and poetic life, was as far removed from Louis as the sky from the sea, and neither of them possessed the qualities necessary for compromise or tolerance of one another. Gathering her favourites about her, Margaret had pursued the romantic life with her ladies, Louis pursuing the violent existence he adored. Soon there was talk that Margaret received more than readings of poetry from such as Jean d'Estouteville, Sire de Blainville, and Alain Chartier, the poet, and Louis' revulsion for his wife had escalated. When she fell sick of a chill and developed the lung flux he had been delighted. By August 16, 1445, she was dead, and he was free.

Then there was Charlotte, his present wife, whom he himself had selected most carefully. Despite this, she too had been most unsuited to him and to her role as Queen of France. She was fecund, yes, but she displayed an intelligence which he found unacceptable in a woman. Charlotte bored him, for he had no interest in her views; and, to preserve the Crown from such unsavoury scandal as that which had attached to Margaret he kept his second wife in semi-seclusion. She was rarely seen publicly, and her attendants were paid by Louis to report her every word and action to him. Too, she was kept short of money, for women living at subsistence level are less inclined to find opportunity for immorality. Of gowns and books, gems and crowns she had sufficient for her status, but of actual coin she had little. They had a daughter, Anne, who was eight years old, beautiful to look upon, and reassuringly healthy. She would always be Louis' pet.

Then, after his problems with his mother and with his wives, there must be this Vixen of Anjou with her asperity and her avarice! What would befall his plans should haughty Warwick take offence and retreat from their agreement to invade England together? God's Curse upon all women except his cherished and adored daughter!

But, reassuringly, it would seem that Warwick was playing the meek servant, and doing as the Vixen bade him. To Louis' relief, the Earl recited a promise which appeared to be sincere and heartfelt, and the Vixen parcelled up her anger.

But there was more to be said, and what must come next would sway Louis' plans towards success—or defeat.

"Madame, I have a proposition to put to you. We are

united in one great cause, and we all crave success for our venture."

"Aye," Margaret nodded, but warily.

"You have experienced the despair of failure many times . . .?" he paused, allowing this reminder to penetrate Margaret's mind. "Now, with our combined experience and with a cause common to us all we have chance of gaining our objective."

Why was the Spider rambling on like this? thought Margaret. Did he believe her disappointments had addled her wits? If so, he was due for some large amount of dismay! For confrontation—as always—was swelling the courage and determination which marked her out from other women.

"However . . ." Louis smiled, a widening of his lips which was like a grimace of pain, "we are in need of a little substance to bind our alliance. Without it, perforce, we shall break apart like a clay pot which has been rudely fashioned and hastily baked. . . ."

To enforce his point, he lifted up a jug which stood on a table near by and let it fall to the floor. Watching it break, Margaret, Warwick and Oxford shivered a little, seeing their ambitions—and perhaps their own bodies—breaking for want of that binding material which Louis had mentioned. Having broken the jug, and kicked aside the pieces, Louis continued.

"Madame Queen, you have a son. Earl of Warwick, you have a daughter, Anne. Would it not be sweet for them to marry?"

Spiked chills raked across Margaret's flesh. Her precious, princely Edward married to sulky Anne Neville with her podgy cheeks and pious expression? Never Never *Never*! And to what purpose indeed? Tie her son—England's heir—to cunning Warwick's brat, when he might have a wealthy and powerful foreign Princess in his bed within a year or two? Doubting she could speak civilly, Margaret had no course but to listen as Louis spoke on.

"Methinks My Lord of Warwick will be greatly successful at securing the Throne for your son, Madame, when that act will also ensure a Throne and a Crown for his daughter. By this marriage there will be a badge of success pinned upon our cause." His bony hand gestured towards the religious badges affixed to his hat.

Margaret searched for her voice, found it, and spat, "*Never! I forbid it! My son is to marry Elizabeth of York!*" And then she could do naught but squirm before the startled expressions on the faces of her would-be allies. Why, in God's Name had she mentioned marriage with Edward Fourth's daughter when such a union would be anathema to her, and *had never even been proposed*? But she was saved the embarrassment of having to submit details of this unusual union, for the startled expressions had given way to ones of plain disbelief and in Louis' there was a hint of suspicion—as if he believed time had shredded her sanity and she was exhibiting the moonfever similar to that of her demented spouse. Her pride choking her like a stranglehold about her throat, the Queen repeated her words but much of the ferocity was gone from them, and her voice quavered.

* * *

Well, it was done. Louis, surveying himself in a metal handmirror, saw the face of an exultant monarch. If a surfeit of lines had been added to his face by the Vixen of Anjou with her insolent pride and her intractable temperament then they were well purchased! He would not forget this summer for many a year, the heat, the turmoil, the wrangling with Warwick, the violent confrontations with the Vixen, the nights when he stayed wakeful and wretched fearing his goal lost because of a madwoman who would not see sense, the days when he believed she would agree to the marriage—only for her to prove even more obdurate at the next interview. But now—finally—she had given her word, and his plan had been aided by the birth of his son, the Dauphin Charles, who was to have as his godfather the Vixen's son Edward. Margaret had been impressed by this honour—as well she might! And that, combined with the luxuries of life at his court had effected to destroy her resistance. However, she had declared her son would remain safe at her side in France until Warwick had captured England. This would prove of little intereference with Louis' plans, and so the bond had been agreed between them, and

Margaret found herself *protégée* of the King of France until she sat again upon her own Throne. Louis had promised to support her and her retinue, her son and his new wife and their train, and Warwick's ladies, until all was propitious for their return to England. And as part of the bond, at Warwick's request, Clarence was to be given back his lands, inherit the Dukedom of York, and be named heir to the Throne until Edward and Anne produced a son.

July 25 had seen the formal betrothal of sullen Anne Neville and conceited Edward of Lancaster (he liked them not at all) after which the Vixen and Warwick had sworn upon a fragment of the True Cross, Louis and his brother Charles doing likewise.

Word of the betrothal and the sacred pact had flared to all the courts in Christendom, and from Burgundy had come a rhyme which had made Louis chuckle.

The King had met indeed
In Warwick his true kin;
This pair—who runs may read—
Were brothers under the skin.

It was not the first piece of doggerel concerning either the Earl or the King of France, and it would not be the last. That the rhymes which were meant to be scurrilous and offensive caused Louis amusement would remain unknown to their composers!

July had dwindled, the days thrusting into August, and Louis had heard of Warwick's frantic efforts to placate his troops. They, glowering and grumbling, saw summer passing while they waited, waited, waited, craving all the while for the joy of battle and its consequent rewards. Jean Bourré, Louis' servant, had parted with four thousand crowns to pay off the disgruntled troops, but now Warwick expected more. There was no alternative but to agree, and Bourré had been informed thus. Louis himself, under cover of making pilgrimage, planned to travel to Avranches and from there make for the coast to talk with the Earl.

The reason for the delay was the blockade set up around the Earl's ships. Burgundians, and a few English vessels had ridden in upon them some weeks before and they were trapped in an impotent cluster. Despite the attendant fleet of the Bastard, Falconberg—Thomas Neville—Warwick's ships would need an act of God to free them.

That act came soon after Louis' arrival at the coast. A sudden storm, violent and destructive, decimated the Burgundian fleet and, on September Ninth, Warwick and Bourbon, Clarence and Oxford scuttled out from their moorings like giant land crabs, some sixty vessels comprising their fleet. Four days later, they were laying anchor in Devon, and Jasper Tudor—son of the fair Catherine de Valois—was galloping to rouse the Welsh to Warwick's cause, other couriers doing likewise to rally Lancastrians and all followers of the Earl. Meanwhile, in France, pearly-skinned with fear and anticipation, Louis the Spider spent his days upon his angular knees begging for Heaven's support for his plans.

He had done all that was possible upon earth; now it was God's turn.

THE EARWIG IN THE ROSE,
13th Sept. 1470–Holy Thursday, 1471

I have no desire to write at length upon that period when the noisome earwig sat entrenched inside the White Rose of York, save to say that I, Edward, was tipped from my Throne by Warwick and Louis and their greedy crew, and mad, mooncrazed Henry Six slouched upon that Throne, his dullard's face gawping from beneath the Crown of England—*my* Crown, jewelled flamboyantly, luxuriant with ermine, wasted upon *his* narrow, scraggy head, sitting upon *his* lank and stinking hair! How it sickened me, and how my Elizabeth wept at thought of it!

They, the traitors, landed in Devon like a band of greasy, murderous brigands, their hearts set upon rapine and booty, and the dethroning of myself, Edward of York. Warwick had old allies, the Kentish men, and with them conjoined Stanley and Shrewsbury, the Courtenays, and those traitors of old, Oxford, Pembroke and my unvaliant brother, Clarence, the Welsh roused by Tudor, the Devonshire Lancastrians, and many others. And within hours of landing, Warwick was issuing proclamations as though he had ever been King, pronouncing all men pardoned except 'King Henry's capital enemies', on condition they rode with Warwick and Clarence and assisted in the freeing of the mad one from his prison. News was brought me that the traitors had entered Coventry with a massive following of some 30,000 men, and I on my way from York sent courier to John Neville, Marquis of Montagu, who was at Pontefract with his men.

Now was there vast disloyalty. Neville, Warwick's brother, had sported the title of Earl of Northumberland while its rightful owner—Harry Percy—languished aprison. I had righted this, giving Neville a Marquisate in its place. He had seemed full happy at this, but now his discontent flared. Abroad from Pontefract, the Marquis rounded on his men, letting words of foul bitterness issue from his lips.

"Edward of York stole my Earldom from me!" he cried

to his followers. "And thereby he has lost him my fidelity! I am no longer great Earl but minute Marquis, and I shall not ride with Edward of York this day! Who is he, this Edward? His Crowning has brought insurrection, his family threads itself through England like strangling weed! And *what* has he? Only a 'pie's nest to maintain his estate with, for all he has is stolen!"

Enraged, I heard of his traitor's speech, and news of the thousands who had risen to Warwick's cause, then we, Richard, my brother, Earl Rivers, and Lord Hastings, with our faithful few made flee for the coast and safety. On October Second we reached Burgundy and my sister's court, there being ensured of loyalty, love, and harbour.

I was weary, a sick tiredness seeping through my flesh and bones like invidious poison. Did no man want me King? Was I then so foul and faulty a beast that I would be better slain?

But my Elizabeth's words rang in my ears. "England is but a suckling babe, my beloved! And like a babe she turns her hungry head towards the proffered breast, but if that breast be filled with poison she will have drunk deep of it before she knows. Warwick is the poisoned milk which England will sup, for she knows no better at this time—poor, foolish damsel."

"A poisoned England?" I said. "What then, my love?"

"Poisons have antidotes, do they not my husband?"

"Aye, that is true."

"And what is the antidote to the Warlock's foul brew?"

I had frowned, not knowing which way her thoughts wended.

"There is an antidote, my love." She smiled, that sweet, fragile smile I adore. "And it is you, my husband, Edward Fourth, the most handsome, brilliant and valiant monarch England has known." Worship had gleamed from her eyes and, her hands crossed tenderly above her stomach . . . which cosseted in its womb our hoped-for heir . . . she had looked as radiant and ethereal as the Madonna herself. Absorbed in my love for her, and my own worship of her beauty and her wit, the anguish of Warwick's rebellion—my brother's defection and duplicity—all diminished. Elizabeth had always had this gift, causing my troubles to shrink, my fears to fade just by her proximity. We are greatly fortunate, for how many Kings and Queens may experience love—and that for one another? Perhaps Edward First and his Eleanor, and Edward Third and his Philippa, yet even they, I think, did not love as intensely and enduringly as Elizabeth and I. Yes, I have had mistresses, and no doubt shall have more, but they were momentary, transient affairs, and no woman—however exceptional, however lovely—could topple my Queen in my affections.

But I was speaking of the vile Warlock's rebellion and my flight to Burgundy. Elizabeth and I had planned carefully regarding her course of action should I be killed in battle, or taken prisoner. She and our family would immediately enter the Tower—should they not be resident there already—and this formidable Palace would harbour them, for it could withstand onslaught and siege of great degree. And so, when I stepped onto my sister's shores, I knew Elizabeth would be safe ensconced within the Tower with our children, yet nevertheless I feared for her. She was with child, and she would be racked for want of news of me. (However, fearing that our son and heir would be born with Warwick entrenched in the city itself, Elizabeth crept from the Tower and took our children to Westminster and its massive, indomitable Sanctuary. There she waited, sending messages to the Mayor of London and his men begging them to remain loyal and hold the Tower for their rightful Yorkist King, but they, mere mortals, meekly allowed Warwick to commandeer the fortress.)

Sequestered in my sister's court, I heard the events of later weeks at second hand, which disturbed me greatly, it seeming to me that since the uprisings and rebellions of recent months had begun I had been overfed with second- and third-hand news. Warwick and turncoat Clarence pranced through my London as if they were right Royal Kings, donning ermine and gems, waving regally to the populace, issuing declarations and proclamations in rich profusion, and then bringing bemused, bewildered Henry Six from his cell, garbing him in crown, jewels and robe of blue, and leading him through the city streets. Blinking in the unfamiliar light, mad Harry was pronounced 'Henry VI, King of England' and I was termed 'usurper, oppressor and destroyer'. Repercussions sprang into being. Calais, where Warwick had once been beloved Captain, snatched my emblems from its banners and replaced them with his—the Bear and Ragged Staff; Dr William Goddard, influential preacher, told his audience that Henry was rightful monarch of England; Sir Geoffrey Gate, Warwick's minion—no doubt possessed of temporary insanity—gave orders that the criminals in Southwark jail—and all other jails—be freed providing they were loyal to Warwick. Meanwhile, those who had concealed themselves in various sanctuaries (for their misdemeanours would have meant severe penalties had they walked free abroad without the Church's benevolence) poured into the streets rife for repetition of their crimes. Looting, rape, the firing and destroying of houses and buildings followed; the streets were crammed with drunken, violent men attempting to enter the city itself but finding its gates slammed shut in their filthy, haggard faces. So, while madness reigned, the King of Madness himself was taken from the Tower, paraded through Cheapside and brought to St Paul's, his leper-white face a mindless mask.

And so a mad King ruled in name, while voracious Warwick accompanied him everywhere, never departing his side, watching, alert and shrewd, as those who professed loyalty approached the madman and made obeisance to him. Shortly, Jasper Tudor was created Lord Lieutenant of Wales, Warwick's other minions taking the posts of Treasurer, Chancellor, and Privy Seal, Clarence becoming Lord Lieutenant of Ireland (Lord Lieutenant where he had hoped to become King! Small sop indeed!). How loudly and how frequently had Warwick denounced my Queen for creating her relatives and friends Lords and Ladies and ministers, yet he, hypocrite-Earl, did likewise when opportunity was given him! His brothers and his friends took premier positions in England, and, on 26th November Warwick was declared the King's Lord Protector.

But, before that noisome day, on November Second, after an arduous and agonising labour, my Elizabeth bore our first son, Edward, and had him baptised 'Prince Edward of England' within a very short time. Our son birthed in a Sanctuary . . . which was but a church-prison . . . with insufficient coins to render him a regal and luxurious baptism! Our son for whom we had waited so many years, and his father exiled, his mother aprison, and England under Satan's rule!

His birth was deemed a great omen by all Yorkists. If mad Harry reigned now, who would come after him? Edward of Lancaster, harsh and arrogant, his son in name but thought by many to be Margaret of Anjou's bastard? Or Clarence, sulky, pasty-faced, a proved turncoat and drunkard? No! More like it would be me, and my handsome, healthy son after me and, if that were the case, reasoned the people, why offend the future King and his heir? My Edward's birthing was the panacea for England's problems, the cure for Warwick's leprous deeds, the springing anew of the White Rose of York. When I heard of his safe delivery I wept, rendering gratitude to God and the Virgin who had protected my Queen through her lonely travail.

Enlivened by this news, I could turn my attention fully to what was necessary, and that was the *coup* I must bring about full soon to get me back my Crown.

My sister Margaret's husband Charles, Duke of Burgundy,* was deemed as handsome and beauteous a man as ever lived; his dark-silk hair shone, his dark eyebrows seemed carefully sculpted upon his brow, his mouth was sensual and curvaceous, and it was full obvious that my sister, his Duchess, cherished the very finger bowl in which he dipped his slender hands after dining. And it was in her that my hopes resided. Now that England was on bussing terms with France, war betwixt Burgundy and France was inevitable, a treaty having been signed to that end, and Charles, splendid, sensual, impetuous, was the boar trapped in the thicket betwixt the two. He allowed me some 500 crowns each month for my household, and he was full generous with his smiles and brotherly back slapping but there—it seemed—the matter ended. However, Margaret, radiant and in the rich bloom of her twenty-fifth year, had a winning way with her husband. I remembered her manipulatory skills from our early years and, as then, they continued to astonish me. Curving an arm through Charles's, she would prattle joyfully of when I was back upon my Throne, and how that

* See Historical Note 5.

day would come swiftly with Charles's help, never by one gesture suggesting that her husband would not proffer gold and men-at-arms to regain me my Throne in right speedy time. Charles, as she painted him, was a good, generous loyal fellow, and family ties meant much to him, especially that family joined to him by his marriage with the King of England's sister. How could the poor fellow have slipped from the gordian knot she had tied about him so skilfully without hurting her bitterly and greatly offending her family?

So, whilst Charles schemed with me, he showed a neutral face to those representatives of Warwick and Louis who made contact with him and they, appeased, departed content. And then Louis by his own haste and greed gave my cause the very impetus it needed. . . . His open declaration of war upon Burgundy and the threatening proximity of his troops caused Charles to reveal his true intentions and, within short breathing space, I had 50,000 guilders in my hands as gift from Burgundy plus four ships to bear me back to England, with fourteen vessels available for hiring should I need them.

As the days progressed towards spring, 1471, more positive did I become of England's need of me. The Vixen and her pup had remained skulking, fearful and hesitant, in France, revulsion and abhorrence of their old enemy Warwick causing this. Had they journeyed to England and shown themselves, she distressed and beautiful Queen, he comely son, they might well have gained such a powerful and besotted following that my cause would have been lost for ever. (For Margaret was a skilful actress, convincing and alert regarding which role to assume for her greatest benefit and, unaware that beneath her son's pretty face lurked a sadistic and callow youth, my people might have pronounced devotion for them both. That would have been my disaster—and England's doom. But, employing an unusual caution, Margaret refused to travel to London, and that as far as I could see was all in my favour.)

How they carefully made their traps and plummeted into them! Margaret showing her distrust of Warwick and England, and thereby losing allies; Louis leaping into open war with Burgundy and bringing Charles and myself closer together; Warwick making treaty with the French, which caused French ships and men-at-arms to cram themselves into Calais and those waters dangerously near England. (Warwick for all his wit and scheming never comprehended the English detestation of all things French, which had developed and grown strongly since Edward Third's efforts to gain the French Crown for himself through his mother's line. Now my people saw Frenchmen lusting for war upon their very doorstep, and they shuddered with revulsion. Too, there was the very fact of a new war, and my people were weary of large scale battle, its bloodiness, its horrors, its savagery. Time now for them to recall our own violent Wars between Lancaster and York, when the White Rose was bloodied by gory petals from the Red. Time now for them to remember latter days when the White Rose had turned upon the Red, stripping off its bloodied petals and thereby gaining freedom to purify England.)

My spies, reaching Burgundy, told me of the people's discontent at 'King' Warwick, who pranced about like a monarch of the Blood Royal—which brewed much discontent and criticism. We English have ever abhorred those who, birthed in the rushes, would seek to sit upon a Throne and thus was Warwick, advancing in years and strewed with a desperation to greedily acquire all he craved before Death besieged him. Lord Protector of England—a grandiose title, the people muttered, but Protector from what....? Edward Four, our valiant young King now separated from his wife and newborn son, or French Margaret who refused to return to our country with her son? Or Spider Louis, whose ships and men-at-arms even now crowded into Calais and English waters under pretence of warring upon Burgundy? Margaret herself was French was she not? Her son—whoever had sired him—was half-French; and were they not both related to the King of France, who was renowned for his avarice and cunning? And now Warwick—who had thundered loud and long that all he desired was England's good—was in league with loathsome Louis and martian Margaret, and Englishmen—whose losses in France were still a festering sore—were expected to watch while Frenchmen invaded their shores. Next, no doubt, England would be a French possession, an emerald badge pinned to the cap of the Spider King, and who would then be King of England? Daft Harry Six? The boy Prince who was half-French and reputed to be the son of one of Margaret's many lovers? Or Louis XI himself?

St Quentin was now in French hands, and Charles was frantic. No more seconds could be forfeited, for both England's and Burgundy's sake, so with twelve hundred men (three hundred of these Flemish mercenaries) plus gold lavished upon us by merchants of Calais and Flanders whose livelihoods were threatened by the Anglo-French alliance, I boarded the *Antony*.

For over a week, savage seas hindered us, and not until March 11th were we able to raise anchor, after which—so thrustful being the gales—we approached the Norfolk coast within twenty-four hours. We might have set foot in Cromer that eve, but word reached us that Oxford's brother, Thomas de Vere, was purging the town of our followers, and these Yorkists—whatever their thoughts—were petrified of repercussions from de Vere. Local men had been ordered by Warwick to repel, on penalty of death, any attempts we made to land. Furious, my brother Gloucester, Hastings, Say and Rivers accompanied by those vessels carrying the men-at-arms could do naught but put to sea again.

Two days after, gale-beaten and threatened by shipwreck, we had no recourse but to approach land and drop anchor as best we might. Fortune—which is reputed to be feminine—courted me as eagerly as a woman of pulsing flesh, and the *Antony* was blown and buffeted into Ravenspur and that part of the coast which Warwick had neglected to reinforce.

Seeing Elizabeth's joyous face in my mind's eye, I fell to my knees upon English soil and rendered thanks to God for delivery from the storm for myself and those five hundred who landed with me. Yet, when hours crept by and my precious brother failed to join us, the exultation of safe landing in my Kingdom was drained from me like wine from a goblet. Young, devoted Richard, not yet twenty, and possessing every quality which Clarence did not; the repository—so my Elizabeth said—for all that was best in our family after the greatest share had been given me. . . . And now it seemed he was dead, his serious, sweet face puffed by the seas, the wet tendrils of his hair swimming voluptuously as eels in the depths. His life forfeited for my cause, and for my son's inheritance. . . . What would Elizabeth say when she heard? Richard was second only to me in her trust and respect, his grave fidelity having deeply impressed us both. She had said many a time: "Our first son shall be Edward after you, my sweeting, but our next shall be named Richard after brother Gloucester." Richard had known of her plan, and it caused him embarrassed delight. Now he would never see his namesake, never hold my second son at his baptism, never profess loyalty to any of my sons . . . never, in fact, have legitimate sons of his own. . . .

My eyes bleached by tears, I waited, and day fled into night then into day, and night fell again. Surely, I reasoned, he could not still be breathing *now*? "Richard, Richard!" my mind cried. "Why you, my sweetest brother?" Indeed, why Richard when perfidious Clarence continued to walk the earth?

Reproach of God was swelling in my heart when the poppy-cheeked courier arrived from my brother to tell me that he, and three hundred men, had safely landed some twelve miles distant.

"God be given all praise!" I whispered, going down upon my knees in gratitude. No death tidings to carry with me to Elizabeth, no threat of her glowing face being dulled by grief!

15th March brought news of Rivers' safe landing with another 200 men at Powle, and we could count ourselves blessed by Fortune, Fate and God. My Kingdom beckoned, plaintive, pleading: "Deliver me, Edward! Deliver me from Warwick's strangling grip; from France's rapacious claws; from the throttling, paralysing web of the Spider King. . . ."

And in that Kingdom, nursing our son in her comely arms, was my adored wife, whose body I craved despite the numerous Burgundian women who had flung themselves into my bed during my exile. (Time later to ponder why Elizabeth fired me thus; why I never wearied of her; why I sought her counsel and her countenance above all others; why, though I might have a surfeit of female flesh, I was always roused by hers. . . .)

Warwick had succeeded by deceit and trickery, and I had learnt much from him; lessons which were burned into my heart and mind by flaming torches. Joyously, he had been welcomed into England when he had declared his cause was England's good and that he did not seek the downfall of its King but only the removal of England's enemies, England lapping up his tale like a thirsty hound. Now was the time for me to broadcast my tale: I was Duke of York seeking the reinstatement of my Dukedom, desiring above all to serve the King with all fidelity. And—though I despised it—bribery assisted me along the track to London.

At York's gates (my father's own beloved York!) I was refused entry twice, then told that for my father's sake they would allow me in alone if I vowed to make no claim upon the Throne itself. Employing further cunning taught me by Warwick, I beamed and smiled and with a few of my men entered the city, we cheering the King and his son as we rode, a Prince of Wales's feather nodding in my hat (though I wore it for my own son and not for Margaret's as they believed!)

Not one welcoming face did we espy, but only dark glowering gazes and bitter silence and, after we had ridden through the city gates, they were clamped shut tight behind us. Should the citizens of York have mortal design upon me, I could be slain within the minute!

But I had my tongue (which Elizabeth said was enamelled with purest gold) and I had my wits, and I knew the men of York as ably as I knew my own kin. . . . Swiftly, I spoke, reminding them of my father and of his love for them which they had treasured, and I told them of my own love for them, and for England, and how my deep care for our land had brought me here, despite the foulest of dangers and threats and how I stood before them as their Duke and King Henry's most loyal Lord.

No hand was laid upon me; instead, smiles were wrought like cloth being woven before my eyes. But they were wily, these cautious, oaken men of Yorkshire, requiring of me to make formal oath that I did not lust after the Crown.

"But where are the nobles before whom I must swear?" I asked them, gazing round. "Unless you send for the Earl of Northumberland who invited me here—as this letter bearing his seal shows, and send also for other high-ranking nobles, I cannot in honour take the oath. But if you do this, you will have to keep me here at least two more days until they arrive. . . ."

While they consulted amongst themselves, my brother spoke to me of his plans to murder Martin de la Mere—the priest who had been York's spokesman—and take the city by force. But I would have naught of that and so, fearing we would be trapped within the city, Richard brought my horse to our lodgings, I mounted, and we galloped off with due speed through the city gates, embarking upon a circuitous route to London to confuse Montagu, who lurked near by at Pontefract with his men. (I could not guess that he had regretted his perfidy and was even now reluctant to strike against me, for Warwick had no more satiated his ambitions than had I! He was still Marquis only, and had not been made commander within London City itself, which made him wary and rightly so.)

Speed and daring had always rewarded me, so both these were employed for the taking of Leicester and Newark, our ranks being swelled by 600 men brought me by Sir William Parry and Sir James Harrington, and another 6,000 brought by Sir William Stanley. Hastings's men allied with us in their hundreds, billowing out from his lands like Vikings from their longships—and all whipped with the desire to have me back upon my Throne. Joyous, I declared my true reason for being in England, declared openly that none but I was King of this land, and heard no murmur of protest at my pronouncements. It was then I heard news of Warwick's followers having gathered their forces for combat with us, they having reached Newark. We galloped like valkyries to intercept them, and were but three miles away before they knew of our approach. They had no time for consultation nor for assuming a combative position, and promptly retreated, taking horse like children who have seen Herne the Hunter! We were masters of Newark and then of Leicester without one arm being raised against us!

What followed is greatest history—and shall be passed from tongue to tongue long after my death. Panic, confusion, betrayal and cowardice all worked together valiantly for my cause, as did Time. How could Warwick have guessed we would travel so swiftly and so surely? We were at his gates in very short time, he cowering behind them like an evil, crook-backed gnome threatened with punishment from the Queen of the Greenwood herself. No doubt he was puzzling as to how I had travelled at inhuman speed, conquering all before me, and winning all to my side! Raucous and demanding, my men planted themselves outside Warwick's gates and there let rise such clatter and confusion that (no doubt) comparison was made between us and Hell's hordes. There was no lesss a turbulence in my own soul, yet none would have suspected—except perhaps my Elizabeth had she been there. Before me were the gates of Coventry and within them skulked the Warlock himself, the man who had prepared England's Throne for me, had sat me upon it, and then had snatched it from under me without a care as to the repercussions of his act. But he surely must be thinking of those repercussions now, as my herald rode through Coventry's gates taking my challenge to him? A challenge for him to ride without the city walls, into the clamour and magnitude of my army, and there make fight with me until one of us should prove victor....

Warwick the Devil-Fighter was dead, however, for no reply was issued to that challenge; it was as if it had never reached the Earl. One, two, three days dwindled, and still he failed to make rejoinder. Then, eager to be away, we departed Coventry, beginning full march to London, and it was as we marched along the Banbury Road that we met with turncoat Clarence and his army of some four thousand, my army and his pausing eye to eye thereupon to make conference.

My brother George had cheated, deceived and lied, raised his hands against his own family, eschewed the cause of York for that of Lancaster, married my enemy's daughter, lusted after my Crown and Throne, and plotted my death so regularly that it had seemed to be his dominant interest of late—and yet he was my brother, born, birthed of Cis, the Rose of Raby, as was I. We both had been sired by Richard of York; we both had worn the emblem of York in our caps as we rode together in our father's retinue.... Of old I knew that my great weakness was love of my family—for had my Elizabeth not frequently told me this? But indeed I had not thought it weakness until this day when, seeing brother George smiling and bowing before me, I was suffused with that intimate affection which characterises devotion to one's brothers and sisters and parents. There he stood, the jagged unruly thorn embedded in the heart of the White Rose of York—the vicious thorn embedded in my own heart—and yet I could not muster hatred for him, nor lust for his execution. Had he been any other stranger, mercenary, I would have made example of him before the two massed armies, showing what end is reserved for those who betray the House of York.

During the moment before Clarence and I came body to body upon the Banbury Road, faithful Gloucester had mediated betwixt us, going from one to the other with messages and words chosen to have most effect upon this troublous situation. As always, he was loyal, circumspect, forthright yet pacifying, pacifying yet not pampering and, when Clarence and I met, he, George, knelt—meekly enough—at which I raised him up and put my arms about him brotherly-wise, our watching armies seeing that there was peace between us. Shortly, this peace was formally declared that every man might hear, and then came chattering and conviviality, Clarence's men stripping the Red Rose from their collars, and calling "*Vive King Edward!*" I in due time pronouncing pardon for them all, and Clarence revoking his fealty to Margaret and her bastard son.

Charging on towards London, it became apparent to me that however much I rejoiced at Clarence's return to our cause and our family, I could never look upon him soundly again. Love him I could, and grateful was I of his return, but always would there be a minute suspicion—like a small worm wriggling, troublesome, at back of my thoughts when I looked upon him—for he could turn again, not being capable of brother Gloucester's magnificent bounty of fidelity.

Whilst passing through Daventry, we made visit to the church of St Anne, kneeling before its crucifix to render thanks to Heaven. Near to me, on a pillar, was affixed a wooden casket containing a likeness of St Anne herself, fashioned from alabaster. The crucifix before me, I knelt, and then happened a curious thing. As it was Lent, the casket was bolted fast, and would not be opened until Easter, yet when I knelt, the casket burst asunder as if released by saintly fingers, its opening being accompanied by a loud clacking noise, and its bolt breaking in two halves. Then, as mysteriously as it had opened, the casket shut. Inside, as all had seen, lay the statue of St Anne which had seemed to glow as if lit from within by tapers.

For weeks men would talk of it. For hours it would remain uppermost in my thoughts. It was the signal I had needed—the approval of Heaven openly displayed; God was smiling upon my venture, and upon the House of York. Naught else could have swayed the people so fervently back to me, for how could they not support God's approved cause? There were men who recalled the triple suns which had appeared before the Battle of Mortimer's Cross when I had been victorious, and many to say that England had offended God by repulsing Edward of York upon whom He smiled—and that England had been as much in error as the Israelites who had taken to themselves a false idol in the desert . . . the false idol here having been Warwick.

So, lauded and cheered, we made onwards for London where so much awaited me: my wife, my son, my Crown, my Throne; my very destiny. . . .

A verse was made for it, that raptured moment when Edward my Husband and King returned to London. The poet wrote:

'The King comforted the Queen and other ladies eke.
His sweet baby full tenderly he did kiss.
The young Prince he beheld and in his arms did bear.
Thus his bale turned him to bliss.*
After sorrow joy, by the course of the world is.
The sight of his babies released part of his woe.
Thus the will of God in everything is do.'

There were songs made for it, too, and couplets and rhymes, but that one I preferred. It said all that should be said, simply and without preamble.

Our son was four and a half months old when Edward took London for his own again, a goodly babe, bliss-cheeked, hair like gilded fern fronds upon his velvet head. He rarely cried, and that had been a blessing in the last few months. My women had told me how tranquil were boys compared with discontented, restless girls, and they had been proved right. Little Edward knew me swiftly, and was given to smiling at those who attended him. Naturally, deprived of my husband, I spent more time with this babe than with the girls hoping, perhaps, to cushion him by my presence, yet knowing deep within that he could not possibly know his father's plight. My attentions were rewarded, for a special relationship bloomed between us which I had not experienced quite like this with my daughters (and would not do so with Richard when he was born).

Hearing of my husband's proximity in London, I and my retinue travelled to Westminster Palace where we could greet the King lavishly and there we waited, by turns tense, confident, and low in spirit. We had not been idle in our retreat; we had designed and sewn many new gowns, ripping

* gloom; misery; balefulness.

apart old ones and employing scraps of material to camouflage their discrepancies. Thus, when Edward arrived, I was wearing a gown of azure blue velvet, low necked and high waisted, with trailing sleeves of cloth of gold embroidered with blue silks, a sash of gold brocade and blue velvet entwined like a young girl's tresses, and the skirt slit to reveal an undergown of azure brocade sewn with strips of silk coloured in Garter blue. Five outfashioned gowns had gone into its composition, yet none would have suspected it. My daughters wore white, each one looking like a Rose of York, Elizabeth at six possessing skin almost as white as our emblem, her hair corn-gilt. Bodices of ivory satin, velvet and brocade had been sewn to skirts velvet hemmed with coney and marten stripped from two of my old cloaks. Elizabeth's sleeves were as voluminous as mine, reaching to the hem of her gown, their linings primrose yellow. Mary and Cecily had sleeve-linings of watered green and cornflower blue, and my precious son was attired in Burgundian silk—milky and sheened like satin, his pink and ivory face bubbling with smiles.

And then the most handsome King who ever took breath stood before us, anxious yet joyful, clasping me tight in his arms, then scooping up our daughters each in turn and looking down upon our son, the heir to England's Crown.

"Edward Fifth . . ." he breathed, absorbing every detail of our son's face as if he feared the child would vanish like a Will o' the wisp.

"Not the Fifth, my husband!" I exclaimed. "Edward Fourth has yet a lifetime before him!"

Edward gazed upon me more closely then, I seeing the anxiety slip from his face to be replaced by desire—and love—and it was then that the entirety of the world receded—even our son—and we were alone in that chamber with but one thought between us.

Later, our attendants dismissed, our lusts satisfied, Edward told me of the bloodless battle to regain his Crown.

"Not one weapon was raised, my precious! No man stood against us—not even Warwick! To strengthen their cause, the Lancastrians even paraded Mad Harry through the London streets but I'm told this so dejected the citizens that they immediately rallied to our cause!"

"They say Mad Harry is a scarecrow without straw to fill his flesh; that his face is a skull, death-smitten and devoid of hue." I shuddered.

"So it would seem, my darling, for he put fright into the Londoners and they are sturdy folk. There is no talk now of the Saint, Harry—all that is forgotten. A weak King has become synonymous with invasion by the French. . . ." He paused to buss me and I snuggled into his arms. "Then news came of George's change of heart, and the citizens realised they were cheering the wrong cause. Mayor Verney and his men promptly sent me a message that I would be welcomed in London, and that I would discover the Tower held in my name, and Aldersgate too. So it was but a journey here from St Albans, and into your bed my sweeting. . . ." Edward grinned, rolled over, and pressed me into the pillows.

"You too have had a great journeying for a pretty girl . . ." he whispered in my ear teasingly.

"The mother of your son. . . ." I smiled.

"No need to remind me, Your Highness! The mother of England's heir . . ." We looked deep into one another's eyes, proudly, dotingly, and my heart thudded with joy.

We were together again; we were reigning sovereigns again; our children were safe; our love flourished like our own White Rose of York. What more could I ask of life than this treasure ladled so freely into my lap on this bright day?

Then Edward slid his hand across my breasts and down towards my thighs, and I gave him welcome to my body. . . .

'THE MERRIEST CONCUBINE': Jane Shore, 1483

I am called Jane Shore, and I have corn-gilt hair which was beloved of the late King Edward, and grey eyes set in a circular face. I was the favourite mistress of King Edward Fourth, the most brilliant monarch England has seen, and he called me the merriest of his concubines.

I must pause now to weep for, though I was merry whilst he lived and cherished me, a great sadness has come upon me since his death this April. He was a mere forty-one—and naught of illness could I see in him, yet suddenly and unhappily for me he died, leaving little Edward Fifth King of England and he but thirteen years of age. Another boy King like Mad Harry! What will become of him? Gloucester preens himself as Protector of our land, but there is a new glitter in his eye and I like it not. They say he has discovered the late King married one Eleanor Butler before he married Elizabeth Wydville and therefore the ten children Queen Elizabeth gave him are bastards and Edward and Richard, his two living sons, are not like to inherit. Will Gloucester be King then? I like it not.

So much discordant and unruly in the past—and so hard a battle did Edward have to keep his Throne. Yet after Warwick was slain in 1471, at the Battle of Barnet (he having marched toward London to attack the newly-ensconced Edward) there was a great peace. He must have been a vicious man, Earl Warwick, vicious and avaricious. Slain, he could harm no one, and yet King Edward regretted his death—as he regretted the loss of any friend or relative, for he had a warm and loving heart.

Others died, too, mostly in bitter battle, like Margaret the Vixen's son, slain at Tewkesbury, Duke Clarence's name beseechingly upon his lips. And some were executed by Duke Gloucester after battle ceased, like Hampden, Langstruther the Prior of St John's, Somerset and Devon (these executions being arranged by Gloucester despite the King having pardoned these men). Why did Duke Gloucester's true nature not appear visible to Edward before his death?

Why was he, of all men, left in charge of the Royal family? But Edward was ever temperate where his relatives were concerned, seeing them as through a roseate haze, and most especially Richard who was as gold beside Clarence's dross.

Then, it was time for Mad Harry to journey to that Heaven which he had attempted to create upon earth, and of his departing I know little. I am but a woman, and a merry one, and death appeals to me not. Save to say Mad Harry died, and with his going my Edward was thrice a King. The mad one's body was found in his Tower cell, stiff and chilled, as if he had been dead a great while and not a mere day, and this white breathless corpse was displayed to the people at St Paul's that they might see he was truly dead.

'That scolding woman,' as Edward's father used to call the Vixen of Anjou, was placed within the Tower (for she had journeyed to London, battle bent, to reclaim her Throne, her cause being lost and with it her one-time Throne) and from there she was 'prisoned in one place after another for four years, finally being restrained at the Duchess of Suffolk's house. In the end, she was ransomed for some fifty thousand pounds, after taking oath that she would give gift to Spider Louis of her inheritances in Lorraine, Provence and Anjou, and would not again lay claim to England's Crown. (I heard tell she died a year ago, aged fifty-two, and is buried in the Cathedral at Angers. Do animals go to Heaven when they die? I doubt this Vixen will!)

Edward's enemies were defeated or retreated one by one —the Bastard of Falconberg, relative of Warwick; Mayor Faunt; even Jasper Tudor, brash Welshman, was driven into exile in Brittany, where he has been this ten or eleven year. Oxford made rapid speed for Paris, where Spider Louis kept him in bread and wine, and peace strode over England with benevolent smiles.

The year before Barnet and Tewkesbury I had first met with King Edward, but circumstance had parted us—which grieved me. Now, right joyously, we were together again and the court at Westminster was become a revel. No grim face nor acid word marred the laughter and the celebration, which clung to our heads as if held firm by unseen hands—and we ladies wore our most fantastic gowns and hennins, great, intricate headdresses steeple-high and wrapt with fine gauze veils which drifted and shimmered like angels' wings. Edward adored the company of his ladies, and to please him necklines were low and breasts pushed up high, waists nipped in, and foreheads shaven smooth and polished until shimmering like satin. Men of our day cherish gold hair upon their women, and the Queen herself has hair which shines like liquid gold, as does her daughter Elizabeth's. (And so have the sweet Princes. Shall I *ever* see them again?) Too, the King's 'most merry concubine' has hair of gold, and thus came a time when women without yellow hair betook themselves to the bleach pot and lightened their dark tresses until they resembled dried straw, crackling and harsh!

Then after the reunion came a grand Royal wedding—that of Duke Gloucester and Warwick's daughter Anne, who were so wrapt in love that they had besought the King for permission to marry. Duke Clarence, greedy and jealous, made much complaint at this, for his wife was Warwick's daughter Isabel and he was not joyous to see Warwick's inheritance shared betwixt him and his brother Richard. Yet marry they did and live in bliss to this day (and Gloucester, despite his temper and his fractious nature, treats his delicate Anne like a saint come to earth; which action is ever in a man's favour).

One man now lay betwixt the King's peace of mind and his son's inheritance and that man was Henry Tudor, in exile with Jasper, his uncle. Henry, son of Margaret Beaufort and Edmund Tudor, had claim to England's Throne through his mother for Lady Beaufort was a direct descendant of John of Gaunt, Edward III's son. (My lover himself laid claim to the Throne from his descent through Edward III's third son, Lionel, Henry Tudor's claim coming to him through a fourth son, but in these vicious, troublous days, all claims must be viewed with great wariness and caution.) The Welsh are infamous for clash and dispute, and Jasper and Henry were exiled in Brittany where the people were Celts like the Welsh. Thus it was not beyond reasoning that Henry Tudor would decide to march upon England, and so Edward employed old tactics—he offered his daughter, the lovely and lovesome Elizabeth, to Henry Tudor, inviting the young man to come to England to collect his bride. However, illness (or pretence of it) kept Henry away and so Elizabeth is still unwed.

England could not summon sufficient affection with which to laud its restored King. He was granted all he desired, money, power, adoration, and soon the court was the most vivid and sumptuous in Christendom, and soon I had much competition—but that never disturbed me! With Hastings as his chief companion and confidant, Edward began to reap himself great reward for the years of soldiery and insult and tribulation, and right glad was I to see him thus: content, great spirited, enjoying his evenings with his radiant women (I was never jealous of any of them), and hunting betimes in the day. At night, Hastings loved to eat sweetmeats—green ginger and the like, washed down with Hippocras and sugared syrups, and Edward would say "I vow thee will have teeth as black and stinking as a well, my friend, if such intent it be of yours to eat a platter of sweetmeats every eve!" and Hastings would make pert reply: "Then I can journey abroad where I wilt and need say no word but smile, for is it not known that we English have the blackest teeth in Christendom because of our love for sugar? So smile shall I and all will say, in whatever language they speak: There goes an Englishman, for his teeth are black!"

"What nonsense you speak!" Edward would chide gently. "Better it would be to wear a placard on your belly saying, 'I am an Englishman, sirrahs'! if thou art so lazy speech is too much effort for thee!"

"And what of those who cannot read, Sire?" I would interrupt. (For I can read and write, where few women can, and love to boast of it.)

"And what of those who cannot read English?" Hastings would say, and then Edward would fill his arms with cushions and bolsters and fling them one after another at his friend as if they were young boys with no cares to weight them. That was how I liked to see my darling Edward, laughing and lighthearted.

It was not hidden to me that Hastings would have enjoyed my body had I allowed him, for he had attempted to abduct me when I lived with Shore, my husband. (He was I wed to at sixteen years of age, whether I liked it or no and

I did not! Seven years I languished as Shore's wife, and then the King saw me at church with my husband and after that I became Royal mistress and my life began anew.)

From the first Edward said "Wear Royal purple, Jane, and make believe you are my Queen!" but he whispered it, for had Elizabeth heard she would have dug her pointed nails deep into my arm and glared at me witch-like, or complained in her fractious high-pitched voice until Edward cosseted his ears with his hands and begged her cease. And so my gowns were shimmering sarcanet in ivory or rich cream, with bodices of sumptuous purple embroidery and funnel-shaped sleeves lined with bright purple velvet and satins. Sometimes, I would don a high-crowned bonnet headdress of purple embroidery over a stiffened cone of purple velvet, or a butterfly headdress of fluttering swaying gauze, but Edward loved me best with my hair streaming free and oft he would pull my cap from off my head and loose my hair with his own hands, burying his face in it and kissing the strands as though he loved each one and dearly. He gave me amethysts and other purplish gems, not all of them valuable and some of them bright-hued glass, but all beauteous and giving me much joy. I had cloaks for chilly days and they were lined with marten and miniver and ermine, and sometimes sable, and many of my gowns were lined with fur for winter as the Palace was a draughty place even with all the hearths a-crackle and Edward's arms lovingly about me.

So would our life together have continued, had not silly witless Oxford begged a few tardy ships and men from Spider Louis and with them made raid upon the English coast, they landing in Essex and marching through England where they captured a castle in Cornwall from whence Oxford despatched his raiders into Cornish lands. Eventually, Edward sent his men to deal with Oxford, which they did, but not before the Spider had sent another two ships to assist him (which were lost at sea, however). From this evil brew, came suspicion of one close to the King—Clarence, who had never ceased to quarrel and complain. Edward believed he had aided Oxford's efforts, and frequently spoke to me of Duke George's looming arrogance. (It would have been better had he never been born, quarrelsome Clarence; he and Duke Gloucester were ever at each other's throats.)

And so time brewed further trouble with France and Edward must prepare for war with the Spider—which he did, but reluctantly, Charles of Burgundy being eager to assist him. However, Charles was as troublesome as Clarence, so when Louis offered to Edward generous terms for peace, and he would have said yea to them, Charles erupted with fury and withdrew his support from England. So rude was he to Edward that my lover would have no more of him, despite Gloucester's attempts at reconciliation betwixt the two. So peace was broadcast and meeting was arranged between my lover and the Spider at Picquigny by the Somme. In cloth of gold Edward greeted the strange and curious Louis, he being garbed in dull and lowly garb, and they talked much, both cautious and yet eager for alliance as their countries needed peace. Then, having reached a point of unity with France, Edward set himself to bettering his Kingdom.

Roads were mires in which men and horses became glued like gnats in spiders' webs, and bands of robbers and brigands lurked at every path's turn, in every copse and wood. Border lands were nests for criminals and thieves, who attacked both pilgrims and straight travellers without regard, whilst in Yorkshire the fractious inhabitants rebelled yet again. Edward rode personally to attend to all these problems, enforcing the local laws, arranging for new roads, despatching Gloucester to put down the Yorkshire trouble brewers. Soon, he was captured by his Kingdom's needs, and I saw no way out ahead; that brief spell of rest and joy after his restoration was broken like a limb in battle.

1477 brought great trouble with Clarence who seemed to have been smitten by a moonfever of fury and malice following his wife's death in childbed the previous year. Her maid, Ankarette, a widow, left their service following that loss and took up abode in Som rset where she would have lived until her natural death had not Clarence decided she was his wife's murderess. By poison in a goblet of ale, Ankarette had slain his wife, so declared the Duke, and the poor widow was dragged from her house, imprisoned in Warwick, and accused of murder. Found guilty, the widow was hanged, and Clarence let further foul accusations slip from his foolish mouth: Queen Elizabeth herself he accused of complicity in the poisoning!

I had never seen Edward as enraged as when Clarence's wild words were repeated to him. His fingers gripped the arms of his chair, the knuckles like polished ivory; his cheeks grew scarlet-hued; his eyes glittered like gems. It was the final dagger thrust from vicious brother George for even one as family-filial as my Edward could not laugh off this insult. Too, Clarence and the Warwick Justices had not the right to apprehend, try and hang such an one as Ankarette—that was the work of the King's own lawmen. And, as though that were not evil enough, it transpired that Clarence was secretly aspiring to the hand of Mary, daughter of his sister Margaret and the late Duke Charles of Burgundy. This triple madness could not be countenanced for, if such as the King's brother behaved thus, then shortly all of England would be in mutiny. Now Clarence took upon himself the most irreverent behaviour, storming hither and thither declaring heatedly that he was loyal to the King and had never sought to injure him or the Queen. Consequently, there was much muttering concerning his irrational behaviour and many to recall Mad Harry Six's mind-flights into a similar wildness. Had the moonfever suffered by that Henry now fruited itself within the mind of another of Edward Third's descendants (for Mad Harry was of Edward Third's line, as was Clarence, one from a fourth son and one from a third)? It seemed as like as not, and many shrank from Clarence, for they had borne a surfeit of the vagaries and tribulations of madness in high places. Beside him, my lover's courage and coolness were like those of a god, and he needed all his coolness when his deranged brother next sought as his wife no less than the King of Scotland's sister Margaret! So, failing to clutch at what he craved via Warwick and the King of France, now greedy George clutched at union with Scotland and, meanwhile, news was brought to court of rebellions in Huntingdon and Cambridge, its leader a man bribed and jettisoned into action by Clarence himself.

Grief warring with fury, my Edward had his unruly brother brought to him at Westminster where he charged him publicly with his offences against England and the Crown, and from which Palace he was then taken to the Tower as prisoner. (Looking on his twisted face, sulkiness seeping from it like sweat, murder bulging from his eyes, I shuddered, stepping closer to my lover. This unnatural, changeling brother should never have been birthed! I thought. 'Twould have been better for us all had he perished in his mother's womb.)

So to the Tower went the most dangerous man in England, his case to be discussed by Parliament, its result being in no doubt and, when Clarence's vile crimes were spoken to his face, men wondered at his brother's patience all these years, they saying "The sooner dead this unnatural son of York, the safer will our country be!"

Other men would have wept when accused, or begged mercy, or confessed all, but violent George astonished every man by lunging into temper's fury, bellowing that he had committed none of the crimes recited to him, and, as though that did not sufficiently stun those watching, he challenged the King my lover to ordeal by combat!

Gulping and gawping, the members of Parliament hastily passed the Bill of Attainder, giving thanks to God that this vicious Duke was clamped in prison. Death was to be the sentence for the man who had plotted so many deaths, not least the King his brother's. Then Parliament spoke loud and firmly to the King, entreating him to have the sentence carried out forthwith, but softling Edward paused, thinking, 'This is my brother, formed from my father's seed, my mother's blood.' And so summer retreated against winter's gale, and February dawned while we at court lived our merry lives, feasting, loving and dancing, singing and sinning with all our energies and it seemed no one had ever heard of Duke Clarence, for no one spoke his name. (Was I the only one to think of him when the wind gusted about the Palace, recalling the chill Tower being washed by the River and blasted by the same winds which gouged at the walls of Westminster? Or did my lover too weep for him in the darkness of his chamber?) I cannot say, but there were new lines about his eyes when February surrendered to March, for changeling George was dead by then, mysteriously, horribly, and no one knew his murderer.

He had always drunk heavily—from his earliest years—that I knew, for many spoke of his unwise imbibing, and then came the news in mid-February—news which shrieked and writhed about the court like moonfevered beldames. The King's brother, who languished in the Tower under sentence of death had died 'of an excess of malvoesie'. That was all we courtiers were told, the very scarcity of detail embroidering a vast tapestry of surmise and scandal, every mouth adding its own stitch, every tongue its different hue of silk. The King's brother had been drowned in a butt of malvoesie, said some, assassins creeping into his cell at night, dragging him wailing from it and thrusting him head-first into the butt of wine until his gurgles and strugglings ceased. Others said that, whilst soaking in his hip bath, the Duke of Clarence was gripped about the shoulders by assailants and plunged deep underneath the waters until he lay still. Yet others muttered that Clarence's worst enemy and rival, Duke Gloucester, had paid men to poison his brother's wine—or mayhap had himself dropped the poison in the wine. However, knowing Gloucester then (as I thought I did) I could not see him performing this quiet, secret deed; Richard was a diplomat, a peacemaker where the realm and his sovereign were concerned—even the Queen cherished him and she was very difficult to please. Yes, Clarence's death would ensure peace in the realm and further secure the Throne, but the stealthy, strangeling manner of it I did not see as Gloucester's work.

So talk of drowning, poison, murder and even of suffocation by pillows from the bed, scuttled about the court and about London itself whilst the body of the dead Duke lay in state upon its bier for thirty-five days, his head then being sliced from his neck and stuck high on a pike on London Bridge. And when the scandal and surmise dwindled to naught—as eventually it must—my lover the King rose from his gloom and there were new-gilded smiles upon his lips. For all that had belonged to Clarence was now his (except some little part which he gifted to Gloucester, and the Norfolk properties which were bestowed upon Prince Richard, the King's second son who was betrothed to the late Duke of Norfolk's daughter, Anne).

Newly-enriched, my King indulged in much which pleased his intelligent and brilliant mind. He purchased many volumes of books, sumptuously coloured and engraved, some of them the entire life's work of the monks who had scripted them, some from Bruges, and some the work of William Caxton, a Westminster man who had invented an intricate and magical machine which did a monk's work in amazingly short time. (For one of this man's books, my lover paid the mighty sum of £20—which I thought overmuch indeed!) Those women who named my lover naught but bed companion, calling him 'the most beautiful man of his time', and cooing at mention of him as though he were a lovesome babe were mayhap loyal enough, but how they irked me, for my lover was a great-minded man, a student and a scholar, and he cherished learning and all that is beauteous. He had the gift of ably absorbing languages, and once studied Greek when he was a prisoner. Too, he superintended the remaking of St George's Chapel at Windsor Palace—a great feat in which were involved England's most expert workers in stone and, while this rebuilding was in progress, my lover garnered a collection of exquisite books and ornaments for the Chapel Library.

Not least was Edward's care for the sea and his seamen. His decision to enlarge the fleet of ships which defended our country gave much needed labour to the shipmakers of England and renewed the country's pride in its sailors—which pride is a healthy state.

Seemingly the years of war were over, conflict within the Royal family now being at its lowest ebb with Clarence dead. But there were other more natural disruptions to interrupt court jollity and the worst of these was the terrible Death, that plague which snatched at all and any man whether he were Lord or labourer. Many who contracted the vile complaint were reduced to skeletons within days—if they survived the rigours of the disease. Most were dead betwixt hours, gross buboes having swelled within their armpits and at their groin, and some developing black spots upon their flesh (it being said that those who showed the black spots never recovered). High, raging fever baked the victims alive, and many spat blood, choking upon the foul flux issuing from their throats and chests, the stench issuing from their bodies being such as to repel even their most devoted relatives and cherished ones. 'Twas not surprising, for the fluids and outpourings of the body assumed a horrifying odour, the urine cloudy, dense and dark, the breath so repugnant as to make those close to the victim retch, or stagger.

At summer's height this blight would cloak us in its stinking horror and trembling with fear we would flee from the city's malodour and its piled corpses, the gaunt faces, the groaning deathcarts heaped with blemished, blood-bespattered bodies. Forcing our terrors to the darkest hidden parts of our minds, we went with the King to Sheen and then to Eltham, and back again, wearing brighter garb and laughing brighter laughs, dancing more energetically and consuming more wine and food—and making love that much more urgently and lustily. 1479 had seen a new daughter, Katherine, born to Queen Elizabeth and this year saw another bout of the Death and our merrymaking far from London's stench.

In 1480—only three years ago—the Duchess of Burgundy, my lover's sister, took it upon herself to visit England, and this gave us high and Royal reason for celebrations, feasting and merry hunting parties. How we ladies ordered and tried on new gowns and headdresses, new gems and slippers, furlined capes and flowing sleeves! Such was the bustle at court that it seemed no one slept by day or night. My gowns were duly selected, in azure brocade sewn with gold silk, emerald silk barred with gold, ivory velvet and brocade, dove silk, gauzy and diaphanous, brilliant samite* threaded with gold, raised purple velvet, satin fugre† in apple green, night blue, perse,‡, sunlight, and marguerite. For lesser occasions I had gowns of baudekin§ and branched velvet, and for meeting the Duchess I wore a sumptuous gown of cyclas,‖ a vibrant purple, and a butterfly headdress of cloth of gold sewn with amethysts. My sleeves were lined with ermine and my slippers were gold

* Rich, gold threaded silk.
† Figured satin.
‡ Bluish-grey.
§ Silk with gold-thread warp.
‖ Rich purple material.

kid, soft and pointed, buckles of amethyst upon their toes. It would have taken a great woman to surpass my garb and appear more queenly and though I do not say the Queen is greater than I, she certainly appeared my equal that day! Her gown was ivory samite, its underskirt azure and cloth of silver, her sleeve-linings cloth of silver bedewed with diamonds, and there were diamonds glittering all about her, upon her long fingers and at her throat. Her hair was styled so that she seemed matronly whilst also virginal, part of it being looped within skeins of gold thread and diamonds and part flowing loose down her back, all being scooped into a voluminous caul of fragile gold netting scattered with diamonds.

Not until late September did the Duchess manage to extricate herself from the joy of my lover's court and sadly did she then depart, tears swimming about her cheeks. Edward had gifted her generously, with ten horses, English wool (famous throughout Christendom) and a splendent riding seat for herself of purple and blue cloth of gold with gold of Venice fringing. So, tears and smiles and embraces over, Margaret was delivered into her ship at Dover and set sail for her marriage land.

To save us sinking into boredom's thrall, the Queen produced yet another daughter the month after, naming her Bridget, and the Scots raided Northumberland as if they owned it, Edward promptly announcing war against them. Their weakling King, James Third, sent word that he had no power to manacle his subjects and if they willed it they would raid where they wished and he could do naught about it. This, my lover thought, was no defence, and the war continued. Yuletide was upon us and with it a surfeit of gaiety, and then came spring, bringing death, for the Princess Mary died at only fifteen, her life flowing from her at Greenwich, her tiny body being swathed in cerecloth and buried in the King's new Chapel at Windsor beside that of Prince George who had expired when a babe. Being absent upon business with the Scots, Edward was unable to attend Mary's funeral, but shortly he returned to superintend the launching of his ships against the unruly, kilted warmongers. Their futile King was so inadequate that there was talk of his younger brother being crowned in his stead, and this brother, Alexander, Duke of Albany, coming to England and meeting up with Duke Gloucester's forces with intent to take the Throne for himself. In Scotland, weak James was put away by his Lords, and Albany created Governor of Edinburgh, after which Gloucester marched for Berwick with his men. But King James was busily planning and sent word to Albany that, if he dropped his claim to the Crown, and renewed his vows of loyalty as a subject, he would be created President of the King's Council and have his estates returned to him. Albany, forfeiting his pact with England and cocking a snook at Gloucester's aid, agreed to this, and shortly he had risen to being Lieutenant of his brother's Kingdom. Startled, Gloucester would have made much complaint but there was to be some reward for his assistance: Berwick was relinquished by the Scots and the Princess Cecilia, thirteen years of age, was to be married to weak James's son, her fate to be the Queen of that gloomy and odious land.

So it seemed we would have peace again but, rejoicing in this thought, I had forgot an even more odious fact: in France there lived and reigned a terrifying, loathsome creature whom men called the Spider King and who, in my mind, I saw as a slimy, repugnant man stinking with decay and draped in foetid rags (for talk had it that he wore old clothes, cared not for his appearance nor for cleanliness, and skulked in corners like a bulging, hirsute spider). This beastlike sovereign, Louis XI who, I was told, had never proved true to anyone or anything, was now turning tail upon the Treaty of Picquigny between my land and his. Louis' son, the Dauphin, was intended for the Princess Elizabeth, my lover's eldest daughter (and how proud Edward had been at thought of having a Queen of Scotland and a Queen of France amongst his daughters), but Louis now designed to marry his son Charles to the daughter of the late Duchess of Burgundy. Charles was seven and the Duchess Mary no less than nineteen!

My lover, ever ablaze with family affection, was deeply grieved at this slight to his beloved and beautiful Elizabeth. And so were all Englishmen, for she was not a babe in cradle knowing naught of this rejection. Her age was sixteen—a time when every pain and every tribulation is triply agonising. To cull some respite from his grief, Edward pronounced war upon France, his daughter's shameful treatment being given as cause. And, being fully behind him, for they loved their fair Princess, Parliament supported Edward's plans and financed his scheme and he, eager for sufficient money to ensure success, began to practise an uncharacteristic mode of economy, both with his family and his court.

While I too longed for the sad Princess to be avenged, it saddened me that my lover would go a-warring again and that the court would be reduced to penny pinching and ale drinking. How could we in all fairness romp and disport ourselves when the King's cherished daughter wept and would hide herself away in her chamber? I myself was sunk in an unusual misery for my lover had been mourning much of late, first for his daughter Mary, then for his sister Margaret, the late Duchess of Burgundy and now for his Elizabeth's shaming. And soon to be added to the court's gloom was the death of Prince Richard's betrothed, Anne, daughter of the Duke of Norfolk, she being given a splendent funeral equalling that of a King's daughter.

Meanwhile, much to my delight, I found my lover did not plan to fight the French himself, nor march to the border betwixt Scotland and England to deal with the savage Scots (who were as twisty and fickle as French Louis). Sitting beside me in the quiet eve, he told me that he had left London before for battle sport, returning to find traitors and criminals clutching at his Throne, so he would not easily depart again. Others whom he trusted must command his armies upon their courses.

Brushing a hand across his forehead, my lover sighed. "My brother Richard is well loved, and as respected as I. He is to command the army in its battle against Scotland. Later, when I have garnered sufficient gold for the French war, will be time enough to decide who commands the army. Though doubtless it will be Richard again. Who could surpass him?"

Sensing a strange weariness in my lover, I pressed my hand upon his which lay relaxed and open across his knee. He looked down at me, deep into my eyes, entering my body with his gaze as a true lover does. "You know?" he said, and I frowned a little. Seeing my puzzlement he opened his lips as if to continue, then closed them. "No, you do not, my sweeting, and it is better you do not.

"What are you?" he smiled, yet it seemed an effort.

This was a game we had played before, and I knew my answer.

"I am the merriest of your concubines, my dearest Lord." And to prove it, I smiled, dimples indenting my cheeks, though I felt as unlike smiling as did my King. What had he meant? I did not know; even now I am not sure. Was it some portent of his death that issued through his mind? Or was he suffering from some illness which he kept secret even unto death? I know not. Yet, that day, some little time before we spent Yule at Westminster, my lover the King had less than four months to live, and was only forty-one years of age.

It was a surfeit of grief and that guilt which assails those whose loved ones die, which caused me to take up my pen and write this. Knowing that my lover had always delighted in my ability to write and read (which is rare amongst ladies) perhaps drove me to compose this little history of our love when other women would seek the convent's solitude, or make pilgrimage. Instead of religious pursuits—which tend to depress me—I was mindful to write down what I felt and what I believed must be made public.

After that last joyous Yule at Westminster, the banquets, the frolicking, the capers and the acrobats, the scent of decorative greenery and the lash of snow against scarlet cheeks, the singing, the entertainments—but most of all the bedding with my King—there came that time when I must forfeit much of the kissing and embracing, for my lover's thoughts wended towards the French war and preparations for it. He was much enamoured of a new brass gun cast for the battles, and was busy ordering new weapons and such like; all things which failed to interest me one jot. I entertained myself by looking back upon the gaiety and colour of the Yule just passed, remembering the dancing and the loving, the clatter and scent and confusion when some two thousand people gathered for festivities. My lover had worn a gown in a new fashion, Burgundian, which fell to his feet withal and was lined sumptuously with miniver, its shoulders padded, its sleeves wide and trailing. He looked the

King, and he looked the lover. No man has ever been so handsome or so lovesome. No King has ever been so Royal or so adorable. So, clutching to me my valued memories, I waited 'til my lover should weary of war and warring, and come back to my bed.

But he did not—through no fault of his own—for the weeks he had spent in London opening Parliament, discussing the Scots' troubles, and planning his French war, were followed by return to Windsor's peace where, rapidly following upon activity, came illness. It was like seeing a great and beloved oak smitten by lightning. One second he was laughing and striding forth like a soldier, next he was too weak to sit up in his bed and could find comfort only by lying upon his right side. Within hours he was so ill that those who had spoken of his swift return to the heart of his Kingdom at Westminster now must parcel up their thoughts. And glad was I, for my lover sank into such depths of sickness that I could not see his recovery being speedy though I prayed and hoped for it right hard. When I neared his bed, he barely had strength to smile at me and lift his fingers to touch mine. Tears—strangers to me until then—leapt to my eyes and gushed down my cheeks.

"Nay, don't weep my pet," he whispered. "Hastings will care for thee—he has always loved thee."

"I do not want him, Sire," I whispered back, gulping as the tears choked me. "I want *you.*"

Then he seemed so overcome that I regretted showing such emotion and crept, stricken, from his bedside after kissing his forehead and his cheeks as gently as I would a sleeping babe's. Closing the chamber door behind me silently, I heard a voice loud in my ears saying, "*He cannot live! The King is dying. . . .!*" and only later when I lay in my own bed did I know that the voice had been my own, issuing from my lips as if possessed of its own will.

Stunned is the only word I can use to describe my state during the next weeks and even now there is an unreality about my existence. Yes I have wept, and spent waking nights, and forgone food and paced the rushes, yet still my grief is unassuaged. If it were, I could compose myself, and strengthen myself, decide what my next move must be, and make it swiftly and decisively. Before he died, my lover begged his dear friend Hastings to make peace with Dorset, the Queen's eldest son by her first marriage. These two, who celebrated no love for one another, were consumed by rivalry, Dorset supporting his mother against those at court who despised and detested her, calling her avaricious and conniving, and of course supporting the King's cause—and therefore mine. And Hastings—once so close to Edward—but now currying up to Duke Gloucester along with other Lords, Suffolk, Buckingham, Lincoln and their companions—though all the while they were dutiful and loyal to Edward upon the surface. (Poor Edward; despite all this, he truly believed Gloucester to be the one man capable of holding peace and strengthening England, and that Hastings still loved me and would have me cleave unto him for my own safety....)

So my lover died, and the court fell silent. We had expected him to live for another twenty years at least, and now he was gone, the golden, handsome, beloved sovereign who had dragged England from the bloody mire of the conflict between Lancaster and York....

And I am left as chill and numb as a statue of stone upon its pedestal, paralysed with grief and disbelief, and already it seems fifty years ago that Edward Fourth loved me, calling me the merriest of his concubines....

AUTHOR'S NOTE

When Edward IV died, on April 9th, 1483, he left the Kingdom in the care of his brother, Richard of Gloucester, as he left the care of his Queen, Elizabeth, and his children, Elizabeth aged eighteen, Cicely (or Cecilia) aged fifteen, Edward, Prince of Wales, aged thirteen, Richard Duke of York, aged eleven, Anne aged about eight, Katherine, in her fourth year and Bridget in her third year.

Richard of Gloucester, who has been condemned since the Tudors as an evil usurper and murderer of his two young nephews, the Princes in the Tower, was by no means feared or frowned upon in his own day. Shakespeare, writing during Elizabeth First's reign (Elizabeth owing her Throne to the usurpation of her grandfather, Henry Seventh, who killed Richard at Bosworth) could hardly paint Gloucester as a man of noble conscience and high motive. Instead, the unequalness of Richard's shoulders, and his small stature, became that of a hunchback, deformed and repulsive. In Shakespeare's *Richard III* (Act I Scene III) Queen Margaret calls Richard

'Thou elvish-mark'd, abortive, rooting hog!
Thou that wast seal'd in thy nativity
The slave of nature and the son of hell!
Thou slander of thy mother's heavy womb!
Thou loathed issue of thy father's loins!
Thou rag of honour! thou detested—'

In Act IV Scene IV, Richard's own mother says of him,

'Thou camest on earth to make the earth my hell.
A grievous burthen was thy birth to me;
Tetchy and wayward was thy infancy;
Thy school-days frightful, desperate, wild and furious,
Thy prime of manhood daring, bold, and venturous,
Thy age confirm'd, proud, subtle, bloody, treacherous,
More mild, but yet more harmful, kind in hatred:
What comfortable hour canst thou name,
That ever graced me in thy company?'

She goes on to say,

'Bloody thou art, bloody will be thy end,
Shame serves thy life and doth thy death attend.'

Shakespeare has Richard lusting after his fair niece, Princess Elizabeth, and no crime is too foul to be attributed to this perverted assassin! However, in Richard's own era, he was highly respected and beloved, the protector of the country's safety, its commander-in-chief in many battles, the King's ever loyal brother and counsellor. He was quieter and more studious than his brothers, dark haired where they were blond, small where they were tall, and yet possessed of a wiry and determined strength. Determination and shrewdness governed him, as did fidelity and deep, deep care for England's good. He was the peacemaker between King Edward and Clarence, and between others who are given to dispute. He adored his delicate and dark-haired wife, Anne Neville, daughter of the Earl of Warwick, and their delicate son, Edward, who died when small.

The contemporary chronicler, Rous, wrote of Richard's birth: *'At his nativity, the Scorpion was in the ascendant; he came into the world with teeth, and with a head of hair reaching to his shoulders. He was small of stature, with a short face and unequal shoulders, the right being higher than the left.'* A straightforward account, yet, it has been used to malign Richard by his Tudor descendants. Apparently, anyone born with teeth and shoulder length hair and unequal shoulders and a short face is a werewolf and devil combined! Suspect, if any at all, would be Scorpio in the ascendant—which would give a strong and acquisitive nature, highly sexed and fertile, moody, vengeful. However, Richard was born on October 2nd, which makes his sun sign that of Libra, and his nature is far more Libran than Scorpion; the determination, the peacemaking, the caring, the shrewdness, all are Libran qualities—as is loyalty.

Contemporary manuscripts have been twisted to vilify Richard when in fact there is none which condemns him. He did *not* personally thrust his sword through young Edward, son of Margaret of Anjou; nor did he personally place poison in Clarence's wine; nor did he lust after his niece; nor was he hated or mistrusted by his family—the opposite in fact. As to the murders of his nephews in the Tower—there is no proof, no document, no statement which is conclusive evidence of this act. Much of the condemnation of Richard is owed to that gentle man, Sir Thomas More, who criticised him roundly, accusing him of multiple murder and other repugnant acts in his *Life of Richard III*.*

The facts, following the death of Edward Fourth are these:

Edward IV had named his brother Richard as Lord Protector following his death, and it was only to be expected (going on his previous excellent record) that Richard would prove fully worthy of this title. However, when Edward died, Richard was on the Scottish border superintending the war with the Scots. On hearing of the King's sudden death, he arranged for a Requiem Mass to be sung at York, having requested the presence there of the Lords and Ladies of the North. Simultaneously, he took public oath of fealty to the new young King.

Meanwhile, Elizabeth the Queen was urging Parliament to crown her son, and she wrote to Edward (who was at Ludlow) advising him to come to London heavily armed and well guarded, for she had no intention of losing her Edward as Margaret of Anjou had lost hers. But Buckingham and Hastings, supporters of Gloucester, repulsed this idea, fearing the results of the boy King apparently marching upon London with an army, whilst the Lord Protector was absent with his, and they reminded the Queen of Gloucester's avowed devotion to her son. However, on 24th April, the Queen's brother, Lord Rivers, set out from Ludlow with the boy King and heavily armed soldiers amounting to no less than two thousand in numbers, whilst in London, Dorset, the elder of the Queen's two sons from her first marriage, took command of the Tower and issued orders for the preparation of ships to defend their position at sea. Shortly, orders were issued in their names—with no mention of Gloucester's name, despite his being lawful Protector!

When Richard arrived in Northampton on 29th April, he

* More's chief source of information was John Morton, Archbishop of Canterbury in Henry VII's reign. He was Richard's greatest enemy!

was accompanied by six hundred men, all of them garbed in black for the late King—but there was no young King to greet his Protector and guardian (a meeting having been arranged there). By now, the new King and Rivers were at Stony Stratford (where, nineteen years before, Edward IV had married Elizabeth Wydville), and Buckingham, instead, met Richard at that place, with tales of the Wydvilles and their greedy, misdirected dominance. On the spot, Richard summoned a Council, their verdict being that Rivers must be arrested and sent North, while Richard escorted the new King to London. On 4th May, Richard and his charge arrived in the capital to discover the Queen and all her family had entered the sanctuary at Westminster—sanctuary seekers being immune from the law. Richard took his nephew to the Bishop's Palace in St Paul's Churchyard, and he himself stayed at Baynard's Castle, his mother's home—not far from St Paul's—until June 5th when his wife joined him, and they moved into Crosby Place, a house rented from one of London's Aldermen.

In the Patent Rolls of April 21st and May 2nd Richard was named Protector, and there was never any hint of rebellion against his title—except by the Wydvilles.

On June 5th, orders were issued for the young King's coronation, which was to be on the 22nd—and invitations were drawn up and despatched, and the new King's clothes were ordered for the ceremony. All was moving forward swiftly and smoothly, when a Council meeting of 8th June dropped a major bombshell into the proceedings. At that meeting, the Bishop of Bath, Robert Stillington, gave the Council an inflammatory news item.

He had, so he declared, married the late King to Lady Eleonor Butler, daughter of the Earl of Shrewsbury, *before* his marriage to Elizabeth Wydville. Consequently, there was a meeting of Lords to discuss this astounding statement, Stillington giving evidence—accompanied by his witnesses—and Parliament discussed the matter on the 25th.

Soon, rebellion was brewing, and shortly Stanley, Hastings and John Morton, Bishop of Ely, were arrested by Richard, Hastings being executed one week later. (Hastings, who had been Jane Shore's protector since Edward's death. Following his execution, she was taken under the wing of

Dorset—who had long loved her in secret.) Lord Stanley, however, was pardoned—which was tragic, for his going over to the side of Henry VII on Bosworth Field in 1485 caused the downfall and death of Richard.

Morton, Bishop of Ely, was put under house arrest, living to blacken Richard's name for all time through Sir Thomas More.

Then more beheadings : Rivers and his aides-in-rebellion, who had assumed command of London in Richard's absence. And Jane Shore, now repeatedly bereaved of lovers, was ordered to do penance in St Paul's Churchyard, 'no man relieving her'—but this was *not* as is popularly thought mere malice on Richard's part. Jane, loving and unwise, had been tale-bearer and mediator between the Wydvilles and Hastings during the plotting of the past weeks.

Sunday was selected for Jane's day of penitence and, on this day, barefoot and carrying a lighted taper, she walked before a religious procession, leaving, it is said, a trail of blood from her bare feet upon the cobbles. From the Bishop of London's Palace to St Paul's she walked, and was then publicly denounced by Dr Shaw, after which she was left unattended in Whitechapel (which, then, was mainly open country). However, this lovely and loving creature was not to be without a protector for long, and soon Thomas Lynon, future Solicitor-General of Richard III, was requesting Richard's permission to marry her. Permission was not refused, but Richard asked that the marriage take place later. It did not in fact ever take place, and little more is known of Jane except that she spent the last years of her life in destitution, dying in 1527.

The result of Parliament's sitting on the Stillington problem was that an Act was passed (*Titulus Regius*) giving Richard the Throne and Crown of England, and the young Princes, Edward and Richard, were publicly pronounced bastards by Parliament.

Queen Elizabeth, still in sanctuary, was asked to part with her son, Richard, "for his brother required his company, being melancholy without a playfellow", to which she rejoined, "Troweth the Protector—ah, pray God he may prove a Protector !—that the King doth lack a playfellow? Can none be found to play with the King but only his brother, which hath no wish to play because of sickness, as though Princes, so young as they be, could not play without their peers—or children could not play without their kindred, with whom (for the most part) they agree worse than strangers!" However, eventually she capitulated, and gave her remaining son into the care of her brother-in-law, both mother and son heavily weeping at their parting. Thus, young Richard went to the Tower with his brother and so began one of the greatest mysteries of History: what became of the Princes in the Tower?

On July 6, 1483, Richard of Gloucester was crowned King, and reigned wisely and well until the invasion of Henry of Richmond and the Battle of Bosworth Field in 1485 when Richard was brutally slain, Richmond taking the Crown as Henry VII.

Queen Elizabeth remained in sanctuary until March, 1484, when she and her daughters moved to small apartments in Westminster Palace. This move came after King Richard had sworn public oath he would not harm them. The former Queen was now titled Dame Elizabeth Grey, her daughters being reduced to the rank of 'mere private gentlewomen', King Richard fully acknowledging that Elizabeth's marriage to his brother was bigamous.

Following Richard's death at Bosworth in 1485, the new King, Henry VII, reinstated Elizabeth as Queen-Dowager, widow of a King, her daughters once again becoming Princesses. Shortly after, on January 18th, 1486, Henry married the Queen-Dowager's eldest child, the Princess Elizabeth, who was then in her nineteenth year.

There was no love lost between the Queen-Dowager and her son-in-law and, during 1490 Elizabeth retired to the convent of Bermondsey. Eighteen months later, she became seriously ill and died the Friday before Whitsuntide, 1492.

Her mother-in-law, Proud Cis, died on May 31st, 1495, and was buried in the Chancel of the Collegiate at Fotheringay Castle, where her husband Richard of York was buried. This church was destroyed during the Reformation, Proud Cis and her husband being reburied by order of Elizabeth I.

HISTORICAL NOTES

Historical Note 1. The marriage treaty between Charles the Bold (also called 'the Rash'), Count of Charolais and Duke of Burgundy, Count of Burgundy, Flanders and Artois, Lord of Hainault, Luxembourg and Brabant, and Margaret Plantaganet, sister of Edward IV, included the following codicils:

(1) Duke Charles was himself to negotiate for and purchase the Papal dispensation necessary to allow the marriage.

(2) Charles was to receive, in instalments, 200,000 gold crowns from Edward IV.

(3) The bride, Margaret, would not renounce her birth inheritance upon marriage.

(4) Edward would finance the purchase of his sister's trousseau and her journey to Burgundy.

The extortionate terms of this agreement were allowed for two main reasons:

(1) Edward wished to ensure Burgundy remained on favourable terms with him should Louis XI attempt to bribe Burgundy's assistance in future war with England.

(2) Edward would desperately need a strong ally should Margaret the exiled Queen consort with Louis, their combined powers laying siege to England.

Historical Note 2. Louis XI was crowned at Rheims on July 22nd 1461. His early years were spent in heated rebellion against his father, Charles VII, and he spent much of his time in the Duke of Burgundy's court until King Charles's death.

Jean du Port wrote 'When God wishes to chastise a people, He gives them a young King." His words certainly rang true of England and France was similarly unfortunate. When Louis XI inherited the Throne he was 38, and the first adult to become King of France for a century. Charles V was Regent of France at 19, Charles VI became King at 11, and Charles VII at 12.

Historical Note 3. The law of the Salic Franks said that 'concerning Salic land no portion of an inheritance may fall to a woman, but the whole succession to the land passes to the male sex.' However, although 'land' is the operative word here, and not 'Throne', this law was upheld to include 'Throne'. Jeanne, granddaughter of Philippe le Bel, was the first female to be excluded from the Throne because of this law. There were other exclusions in 1322 and 1328.

Historical Note 4. According to French historian, Maurice David-Darnac, Joan of Arc was not in fact burnt at the stake in Rouen in 1431, but was assisted to a place of safety whilst another woman died in the flames. He related that Cauchon, Bishop of Beauvais, helped Joan to escape via a well-shaft in the Château de Bouvreuil, this leading to a subterranean passage. Possibly she then spent some four years in prison, being released in 1435, when the Duke of Bedford died at Rouen. Returning to Lorraine, Joan made contact with the d'Arcs (who, says David-Darnac, were not her real family but foster parents). Others besides the d'Arcs saw Joan and identified her as Jeanne la Pucelle. Joan then attempted to resume her career, but without success, and finally she married Sire Robert des Armoises, spending her last years at his home, Château de Jaulny, and at her own house in Metz. In 1449, she died without having borne any children. These, and other fascinating facts, all impressively substantiated, can be read in *Histoire, Véridique et Merveilleuse de la Pucelle d'Orléans* by Maurice David-Darnac. In the Château de Jaulny, over a fireplace, is a portrait of Jehanne (another medieval spelling of Joan) wife to Robert des Armoises; the portrait is not unlike the one executed by Clement de Fauquemberge.

Historical Note 5. Charles the Rash (or the Bold) was born at Dijon on November 11th, 1433, under the sign of Scorpio. He displayed all the characteristics of Scorpio to a marked degree, being black haired, swarthy skinned, industrious, fiery and rash-tempered, vengeful, strong-willed and sharp-tongued, ambitious, suspicious, arrogant, caustic and callous.

It is interesting, too, to note that Warwick, born under

the sign of Sagittarius, was greatly typical of his sign—an adventurer, proud, restless, ambitious and combative.

Edward IV, born under Taurus, was Venusian to the core: sensual, handsome, indolent, pugnacious and determined in battle, self-indulgent and corpulent in later years, and always highly popular with the opposite sex.

Perhaps Louis XI would have been more aptly named the Crab King. Born under the sign of Cancer, he concealed himself behind a formidable shell, causing confusion and bafflement amongst his enemies; he was avaricious and acquisitive, and kept his foes in order by nipping at their heels when they attempted to overreach themselves. His elusive, sidetracking schemes ensured that his enemies remained greatly in the dark as to his true intentions. This deviousness mingled with a gift for self-preservation and wiliness, tenacity, asperity, an unkind wit, moodiness and critical qualities. Louis' persistent pursuit of his wife Charlotte is typical of a Cancerian; however, her failure to provide him with stimulation, or to keep him interested in her, quashed their relationship at an early point.

BIBLIOGRAPHY

Calmette, Joseph, *The Golden Age of Burgundy*, Weidenfeld & Nicholson (1962).

Champion, Pierre, *Louis XI*, Cassell.

Coryn, M. *House of Orleans*, London (1936).

Davies, Katharine, *The First Queen Elizabeth*, Lovat Dickson Ltd. (1937).

Edwards, William, M.A. *Notes on European History (to 1494)* (Rivingtons, 1964).

Erlanger, Philippe, *Margaret of Anjou*, Elek Books, (1970).

Hamel, Frank, *The Dauphines of France*, Stanley Paul & Co.

Harvey, John, *The Plantagenets*, Fontana.

Kendall, Paul Murray, *Warwick the Kingmaker*, Sphere.

Leary, Francis, *The Golden Longing*, Murray (1960).

Rowse, A. L., *Bosworth Field* (and Wars of the Roses), Macmillan.

Baldwin Smith, Lacey, *This Realm of England, 1399–1688*, D. C. Heath & Co. (Boston).

Stratford, Laurence, B.A., *Edward the Fourth* (London, 1910).

Strickland, Agnes, *Lives of Queens of England*. Coronation of Elizabeth Wydville (London 1935).

Timbs, John, F.S.A., *Curiosities of History* (London, 1881).

Turton, Godfrey, *The Dragon's Breed* (The Tudors), Peter Davies.

A Selection of Historical Fiction from Sphere

THE GAME OF KINGS	Dorothy Dunnett	40p
QUEENS' PLAY	Dorothy Dunnett	40p
THE DISORDERLY KNIGHTS	Dorothy Dunnett	60p
THE BLACK PLANTAGENET	Pamela Bennetts	30p
BORGIA PRINCE	Pamela Bennetts	35p
THE BORGIA BULL	Pamela Bennetts	35p

KATHERINE OF ARAGON	Julia Hamilton	30p
ANNE OF CLEVES	Julia Hamilton	30p
ANNE BOLEYN	Margaret Heys	30p
JANE SEYMOUR	Frances Clark	30p
KATHERINE HOWARD	Jessica Smith	30p
KATHERINE PARR	Jean Evans	30p

The above six titles are also available in an attractive slipcase at £1.80